Where Willows Weep

LUNA FIORE

Blurbs

"Where Willows Weep is a sweltering Southern gothic horror romance that blends the swoony delights of childhood friends-to-lovers and the terror of a haunted house. A perfect read for fans of Mike Flanagan's stories, where the interpersonal might be just as terrifying as the things keeping Jessamine up at night."

-Ladz, author of THE FEALTY OF MONSTERS

"In true gothic fashion, Fiore crafts relationships that stick with you long after the novel has finished. The rot of the Montgomery household is alive and very, very unwell."

-A.A. Fairview, author of TEETH AND TAROT

"In WHERE WILLOWS WEEP, Fiore immaculately captures Southern gothic horror and romance with characters stained in both blood and red clay. At the core of this unnerving story about trauma and survival is a raw, vulnerable, and passionate romance between Jess and Sam. Highly recommended for fans of horror like THE BABADOOK and Mike Flanagan's THE HAUNTING OF HILL HOUSE."

–Morgan Dante, author of PROVIDENCE GIRLS

"Luna Fiore has crafted a ghastly story about Sapphic desire drenched in sticky summer heat that clings to your skin much like the ghosts whispering in your ear do. Where Willows Weep will haunt me for quite some time."

-Ezra Arndt, author of GOD & THE CONQUERED

To my mother, who taught me how to excise the rot from my own roots

Content Warnings

WHERE WILLOWS WEEP is a Southern Gothic horror that has use of marijuana implied/referenced CSA, SA, incest, child loss, miscarriage (past), trauma, transphobia (slurs), churches and touchy pastors, on page consensual sex (between MCs), violence, blood and period blood, mental hospital stay (past), breakdown, questioning sanity, dementia, incontinence, almost drowning, death (past), corpses, wounds and descriptions of infection, vomiting, and body horror.

Chapter 1

TREES BENT AND WAVED, heralding the return of the child that had left them nearly seven years ago. Leaves turned over, showing their light green bellies to greet the rumble of thunder. A sure sign of the storm to come. Jess smelled the crackling ozone in the air. Wisps of her hair whipped out of the open window as she leaned her forehead on the frame. Cold wind mixed with hot air buffeted her skin. An incessant tapping clashed with the crackling of radio static.

"I think it'll be good for you," Celia said, her fingers tapping against the steering wheel. "Momma needs someone to watch over her now and I'm too busy with the kids—"

Jess tuned her out. It was always the same explanation over and over again. Celia had a husband and kids and a household to manage while Jess was the fuck up. She could hear the whispers in church already. Couldn't even make it through college. Couldn't keep a boyfriend.

She'd returned to the small town of Marisville with no husband, no children, and she didn't even have a degree to show for it.

"Jessamine? Are you listening to me?" Celia demanded with a huff.

"Mhm."

She could almost hear Celia roll her eyes. "I really need you to pay attention. Momma needs—"

"We've been over what she needs. I don't need another lecture," Jess snapped. "If you don't think I can do it, you should've hired a nurse or—"

"I'm not putting her into a home," Celia forced out through clenched teeth. "I don't trust those places to take care of her, and besides, we can't afford it."

"You mean to tell me even with your husband's new job that pays so much more than his old one you can't afford a new home for momma but you could afford this new car," Jess sneered, mocking Celia's often haughty tone. The one that pissed Jess off every time she heard it.

The steering wheel creaked under Celia's white knuckles. "I have three children, Jess. Do you have any idea what it takes to provide for three kids?"

"No, but I'm sure you're going to tell me."

"Abby has a cough and Connor might have asthma, and Jake Jr.—"

"I don't care about kids you won't even let me see."

Celia snapped her mouth shut and sighed. "I know you're still angry with me, but what else was I supposed to do? I followed the doctor's recommendation, I don't," —she sighed again— "I don't know what you want from me Jess. I was just trying to do what was best."

"What was best or what was easiest?" Jess grumbled.

Celia didn't answer. She didn't have to. Jess knew the answer before she even asked the question.

She reached in between them and fiddled with the dial on the radio. Static ebbed and flowed as she searched for a channel with some kind of noise. Hell, she would even settle for the scratchy sound of a sermon if it meant she didn't have to talk to Celia again.

Dark clouds followed them as Celia turned down the road, hidden between two tobacco fields, that fed right into main street. The only main street. Nearly everything about Marisville existed on that one street. The diner that everyone went to after church on Sunday, and the ice cream shoppe attached that opened during the summer, the only clothing shop—a middle-aged white woman's dream boutique—unless one wanted to buy their clothes at the church-run thrift store.

The church that had started off as a singular room but full collection plates and monthly tithes paid for new additions to branch off the original building in an off mishmash of angles that made Jess sick if she looked at it too long. The corners were all wrong. Too sharp. A small patch of grass shaded by a few trees separated the church and its thrift store. Jess watched as a woman rolled in a rack of faded clothes through the open glass doors to protect them from the oncoming storm.

Celia drove past the general store and pharmacy where they used to buy packs of gum for a quarter and walk back home while trying to blow the biggest bubble before they popped, covering their mouth and noses with the sticky sweet confection. They always spat out the gum in the trash can outside before going back in the house.

Aveline Montgomery, known to her children only as Ma'am and Momma, did not allow gum in her house lest someone grind it into her carpet and earn themselves an ass whoopin'.

Brick storefronts looked as if they were held together by prayers and sheer force of will. Signs were faded. Letters had disappeared from sign boards. Many neon signs read 'ope' or 'pen' instead of open.

Everything looked exactly as she had left it seven years ago.

Fuck, that's depressin'.

Celia took the road tucked beside the hair salon that only saw the church ladies who needed their curls set for Sunday morning service and small children taken in for haircuts against their will. Jess remembered the god-awful time she sat in that sticky plastic chair while Betty Fisher butchered her hair by giving her bangs 'that were all the rage for kids her age.' Jess had spent most of the school year using a headband to push her bangs back. It didn't always work and left her bangs constantly sticking up even after several rounds with the hair dryer and her momma's round brush.

"Looks like we'll just beat the rain," Celia finally spoke again. "I can stay for the night, make sure you get settled in okay."

Part of Jess wanted to tell Celia to fuck off, but she also didn't want Celia to just drop her off and leave. While Momma's memory wasn't what it used to be—dementia the doctors called it—she just might remember their last conversation before Jess packed her things and took off, leaving Marisville behind in her rearview.

"Okay," Jess murmured.

Pavement turned to dirt. Dust puffed up into a cloud and Jess leaned away, finally rolling up the window. The houses were in just as rough shape as the buildings on main street. Old plaster lath houses with sagging porches and patchy wooden siding. One good wind would knock some of them right over.

Celia parked in a driveway overgrown with weeds. Yellow dandelions sprouted around the tires of an Oldsmobile and grew through the rusted spokes. Sun-faded denim blue paint peeled away from the taillights. Jess would be surprised if the car ran, and she hoped it did otherwise she was trapped unless she found a ride or walked into town. Neither she could do without someone to watch Momma.

Knee-length grass whispered in the wind and tickled her legs. Jess stared up at the two-story house with cracked yellow paint and sagging windows. The world held its breath with her as the ghosts of child Jess giggled while running through the yard and swimming in the pond barely hidden by the thatch of willow trees she and Celia used to climb. Good and bad memories danced around each other, reminding her why she left but also reminding her why it was home.

She released her long held breath. The wind picked up, the rustling grass a welcoming cry. Beetles clicked as they clung to the strands. She flicked one from her leg. Thunder clapped, closer now.

"Your stuff, Jess," Celia reminded, standing by the open trunk with a red duffel bag in hand. "Good thing Momma left our room alone since you don't have much."

Jess couldn't afford much while living on her own and many of her belongings had found their way to the trash before she left. Nearly everything, from her mattress and bedding to some of her clothes felt soiled. Jess had packed what didn't give her a panic attack, some safe clothes and books and notebooks, which didn't leave all that much. Celia hadn't understood but she also didn't say anything while she watched Jess haul bags full of things down to the dumpster.

Old boards creaked under her weight. Dandelions poked up through the gaps of the porch. White paint peeled away from the railing. Everything was on the cusp of falling apart.

An apt way to return home.

The screen door screeched open. A familiar, painted face smiled—pink lipstick smeared on teeth—as Jess took a small step back. As if she bolted for the car, Celia would take her anywhere else. She wouldn't. Jess was stuck here.

"Jess, darlin', look at you!" Nancy Fisher crowed, thick hands pulling Jess into a hug.

Cloying rose perfume assaulted Jess' nostrils, nearly making her sneeze. Nancy pulled away, hands still gripping Jess's arms and keeping her rooted in place, while her painted eyebrows almost melted into her hairline.

"Honey, you got so skinny, have you even been eating?" Nancy didn't wait for an answer. "Baby, don't you worry none, as soon as Celia said you were coming I started cookin' your favorites. Collard greens been on all day, just pulled the biscuits out, and I'm about to start on the dirty rice and smothered pork chops. How does that sound?"

"Sound great," Jess said, and she actually meant it. She wasn't much of a cook and hadn't had a home cooked meal in a long time.

"And of course I brought some hummingbird cake for dessert," Nancy said, holding open the screen door. "Mary down at the church—you remember Mary, don't you?—baked it fresh this morning and dropped it off. Course she couldn't stay on account of her husband's incident—"

Nancy kept chattering away, not caring whether or not anyone was listening, and the moment Jess stepped over the threshold, she wasn't. The stairs to the second floor stretched up in front of her, leading to the closed door of her grandfather's room. After Pawpaw died, Momma kept the room shut up tight and no one was ever allowed to go in.

To the left was the mouth-watering smells of dinner. To the right was the living room where Aveline sat in her recliner, eyes glued to the television, looking nothing like the woman Jess had run away from.

Celia took Jess' duffel. "I'll take these upstairs so you and Momma can talk."

With a hard swallow, Jess turned away from the matching expressions of pity on their faces, and stepped into the living room. Wispy white drapes fluttered in the breeze coming in through the open windows. A window unit sat still and silent in the window right by Momma's faded blue recliner. On top of a cloth-covered buffet was the old box television showing reruns of I Love Lucy. Canned laughter followed Jess across the room.

Aveline Montgomery had been a broad-shouldered woman with a strong jaw and nose, and eyes that could crinkle in the corners as her loud laugh filled the room or blaze with fire as she told her daughters to 'knock their shit off or so help her.' She had been a giant. A pillar of church and community. The first to help even when someone didn't ask for it, and the first to tell someone when they were full of shit.

This wasn't that woman.

The recliner threatened to swallow Aveline whole. She had lost weight. Perhaps even shrunk. Frail arms rested on the arms. Fingers absently picked at a loose thread.

Jess sat down on the edge of the floral green couch, palms skating down the denim of her shorts to wipe away the thin layer of sweat and pressing into her knees. "Momma?"

Aveline didn't look up from the TV. Withered lips moved but Jess didn't hear her say anything. With a shaky hand, Jess leaned forward and rested her hand on her mother's cold skin.

Dark brown eyes finally slid to hers but...they were empty. Aveline stared at Jess with no sense of recognition. A fist squeezed Jess's heart. Gaps in her memory, that was what Celia had said, but nothing to prepare Jess that Momma might not recognize her at all.

"Can I help you, darlin'?" Aveline's voice wavered.

"Momma, it's me, Jess," she said. "I came home."

Aveline stared at her, eyes squinting and mouth pinching at the corners. "Jessamine?"

"Yes," Jess sighed in relief.

"My Jessamine went away to college," Aveline said. "First in our family to go. I'm not sure when she'll be back but you're welcome to wait."

Jess shot up from the couch but Aveline barely noticed, her attention back on the TV. The screen door crashed against the wall and Jess leaned on the railing, knuckles turning white. Her eyes burned. Breath rattled in her lungs.

"It won't always be like that," Celia murmured, leaning onto the railing beside her. "Some days she'll know who you are and some she won't."

"You didn't tell me," Jess softly accused.

Celia huffed. "I tried. I don't think you listened to half of what I said on the drive here."

Jess couldn't argue that.

"Despite what you might think, I wish I could be here too or find a better place for her to stay, somewhere closer to us." Celia ran her fingers through her bottle blond hair, the roots a muddy brown. "I'll call and check in, and we'll come down when we can."

"It's fine, Cel," Jess grumbled though it was far from fine. This wasn't what she had signed up for. None of it was what she had signed up for. Everyone else was making decisions about her life and she was just along for the ride.

"Nancy said she and a few of the other ladies from church will bring meals since everyone knows you're a shit cook—"

Jess coughed a laugh. She liked eating but never much liked cooking and when she was finally interested in learning, there was no one to teach her.

"You won't be alone here. Nearly everyone has volunteered if you need a ride or someone to watch Momma for a short so you can take a break or anything you need to do. I've left all numbers by the phone," Celia kept going as if any of it could fill the growing void in Jess' chest. "While I can't afford a live-in nurse, Derotha will be by three times a week to check up on things and help with bathing and whatnot—"

"This isn't fair," Jess whispered.

Celia fell silent. "No, it isn't," she agreed. "But this is what is. All we can do is take care of her as best as we can."

Jess bowed her head, staring down at the weeds invading underneath the porch.

"It would help to have friends," Celia said. "Maybe you could call up Sam. I'm sure he missed you."

Sam. Jess' high school sweetheart, more like middle school sweetheart, that she hadn't spoken to in years. The last time she had seen him, he had driven her to the bus station a town over and helped her buy a ticket. She had promised to call and write. A promise she had upheld at first, calling nearly every day and writing the odd letter. Every day turned into every other day then once a week, a month, until she stopped altogether.

"I doubt that," Jess said.

Celia shrugged. "You never know."

Jess wasn't going to make friends. These were the people she had run from. They were nice now, volunteering to bring food and help, but their help came at a cost. Whatever help they promised would loom over Jess' head until the day they died. They'd come into the house and then go back to church and gossip about how awful of a daughter she was and how terrible the whole situation was. Sam had hated that as much as her, but Jess had burned that bridge a long time ago even if she hadn't meant to.

"I don't know about you but I'm hungry," Celia said, pulling away from the railing. "Best go inside before Nancy bursts. I'm sure she's itching to tell you everything you've missed in the last seven years."

"Oh God," Jess muttered. "Do I have to pretend to care?"

"It would be polite of you."

Thankfully, her upbringing had prepared her for the sheer number of sympathetic noises she had to make while scarfing down the best meal she had in ages. Nancy spared no detail telling Celia and Jess about every dramatic event that had befallen the small town of Marisville, but with church and community they always managed to find their way back. Jess fought the urge to roll her eyes so many times she lost count. If she had taken shots every time Nancy said, "we prayed for them" or "we asked God for guidance," Jess would've had to go to the hospital two towns over for alcohol poisoning.

Celia had helped Momma walk from her recliner to the kitchen table, her slender fingers wrapped around her cane, and sat her down at the head of the table. All of her food was cut into tiny bite-sized portions to keep her from choking. Jess thought coming home meant keeping Momma company, not taking care of Momma as if she were a child.

"What time should I pick you and Aveline up for church?" Nancy asked, clearing away the empty plates and carrying them to the sink. "Service starts at half past eight, but Reverend Daniels always waits for your momma so if you need a little extra time no one will mind."

"Church?" Jess asked, eyebrow raised, and looked to Celia.

Celia nodded. "Momma is still adamant about going to church on Sundays."

"Never misses a service," Nancy added cheerfully. "In fact, she seems more like her old self on Sunday. I suppose that's just the healing power of God."

Jess rolled her eyes behind Nancy's back and Celia quietly swatted at her arm. "It makes Momma happy so please get her ready and take her," Celia said. "And it'll be good for you."

Nancy carried the cake to the table. "Oh! It will be wonderful for you Jessamine, and everyone will be so happy you're home."

"I'm not sure I have anything to wear," Jess admitted. She hadn't packed any of her Sunday dresses when she fled years ago.

"Don't you worry about that darlin'. Just wear whatever you have and we can find you some nice clothes at the thrift store. Mae's daughter just donated quite a few things and you're about the same size," Nancy reassured her.

Jess poked the cake with her fork, scraping away the spiced cream cheese frosting. "Will the Williams' be there?"

Will Sam be there?

Nancy's smile grew tight. "I...perhaps," she forced out between clenched teeth. "But the Rutherfords' will be there. You remember their son Jonathan? He's running the general store now and I'm sure he'll be very interested in seeing you again."

Celia gave a small shrug when Jess looked at her in confusion. Jonathan Rutherford hadn't paid Jess a damn bit of mind in high school, and she doubted he would be at all interested in seeing her again. And why was Nancy trying to change the subject away from the Williams'? Had something happened to make them leave the church? Or maybe they had no interest in going and possibly seeing her after she left their son high and dry, waiting for a call or letter that never came.

It took a whole hour after the leftovers were put away and the kitchen was cleaned to get Nancy out the door. She'd say goodbye and then suddenly remember something she just had to tell them. By the fifth time, she had finally run out of things to say, and Celia walked her to her car, giving Jess a moment to breathe.

Jess plopped into one of the rocking chairs underneath the living room window and waited for Celia to walk back up the driveway.

"Fuck, I need a beer after that." Celia opened the screen door. "Want one?"

Jess nodded. "She's just as irritatin' as I remember!" Jess called through the open window. "And my god, could barely get a word in edgewise."

Celia emerged on the porch with the beers and sat in the rocking chair beside Jess. "I know," —she stretched her legs out and rested her feet on the railing— "but Nancy helped coordinate the other ladies so someone could stay with Momma until I could figure out something. The woman can't shut up to save her life, but she was here."

Jess held the cold can to her cheek for a moment and huffed. "That's nice and all, but you do know she will never let us forget it, right?"

Celia shrugged as she cracked open her can. "There are worse things to live with."

Mimicking her sister, Jess rested her feet on the railing and leaned back in the rocking chair as it creaked in protest. Humidity clung to her skin. Her roots grew damp. Wisps clung to her neck. She already missed air-conditioned buildings. Coming home meant sweating at night even if she didn't wear a stitch to bed and constantly washing the sweat and oil out of her hair.

Jess took a sip of her beer and grimaced. "God, why is this shit so terrible?"

"It's cheap." Celia giggled. "You remember when Sam and Ben would take us over to Jacksonville and we'd sneak into the bar for nickel beer nights, and it was always PBR."

"Of course," Jess said, smacking a mosquito that had landed on her thigh, smearing the blood across her skin. She wiped her hand on her shirt. "It's the only way they could get rid of that shit."

"It wasn't that bad."

"After three pitchers it wasn't that bad," Jess corrected. "And then one of us, usually you, would have to puke in the bushes before Sam drove us to the diner on the highway so we could sober up before trying to sneak back in."

"I miss those days," Celia sighed wistfully.

"I miss those pancakes."

Celia laughed. "Maybe we should've stopped on the way in."

"I'm not sure it would've made anything better," Jess whispered.

Celia pressed her lips together. "Will you ever let this go?"

The can warped under Jess' tightening grip. "I don't know."

Celia sighed and drank her beer in silence. Any growing sense of camaraderie died as they rocked in silence broken up only by the tinny sound of audience laughter from inside and the distant peals of thunder.

"We should get Momma to bed," Celia finally spoke. "And I'm tuckered out."

Jess hummed in response.

Getting Momma to bed consisted of turning off the television and coaxing her out of her recliner, where she had already started to doze off, and walking down the hall to the only bedroom on the first floor. Momma changed into a soft yellow nightdress and Celia tucked her in underneath the white cotton sheets. A small white device sat on Momma's nightstand and Celia clicked it on before shooing Jess back into the hallway and softly closing the door. She handed a matching device to Jess. A green light flickered.

"A baby monitor," Celia explained. "In case she needs anything or if you hear something odd, you can check on her."

"Oh."

Celia hadn't lied about Momma leaving their room alone. Two twin beds were pressed against opposite walls. One half Celia's and one half Jess'. Though after Celia left in the morning, the room would be all Jess'. Fresh baby blue sheets on her bed smelled of cut grass and honeysuckle. Cheap neon plastic beaded necklaces hung from the white bedpost. Jess flicked them, listening to them swish together. Sam had won them for her during the County Fair playing that ridiculous duck fishing game over and over until he got her one of every color. The stuffed orange cat he had won playing darts sat on her pillow. Jess held the stuffed animal up to her face and breathed deep, hoping some traces of him remained, but the smooth fur and stuffing just smelled like laundry detergent and grass.

"Seriously, Jess, just call him," Celia said, pushing open the window to let in the breeze.

"Maybe," Jess mumbled into the fur. "But what if he hates me?"

"I mean hell could be freezing, I suppose, but if anyone will forgive you, it'll be Sam."

Chapter 2

CRACKLING STATIC JOLTED HER awake. Jess' heart thudded against her sternum while she laid in bed, staring blearily at the barely lit ceiling, trying to get her bearings. She was home. Had been for a few days now. Celia had left that first morning, promising to return when things settled down to visit with the kids in tow but Jess wouldn't hold her breath.

A cough came from the baby monitor on her nightstand and Jess sighed.

Momma woke early. Getting up just after the crack of dawn and Jess had no choice but to get up with her. With the monitor in her hand, Jess stumbled down the stairs. She rubbed her tired eyes with her fist. The door to her mother's room was cracked and Jess gently pushed it open.

"Morning, Momma," she said, her words punctuated with a yawn.

"Don't speak to me and yawn, Jessamine, it's rude," Momma grumbled from where she sat on the side of the bed. "It's time to get ready for service."

Jess paused. That was the first time Momma had known who she was. The last few days she barely spoke to Jess as if she didn't even register Jess' presence beyond eating meals and being tucked into bed at night. "You know who I am?"

"Of course I know who you are." Aveline's dark eyes narrowed at Jess. "My daughter who stormed out of here promising me she would never come back to this shit hole. But I guess that didn't go as planned, did it?"

Jess felt the flicker in her chest. The smallest hint of rage that she shoved back down. "You didn't know who I was the last few days. I was surprised, that's all."

"As if I'd forget I raised such an ungrateful child," Aveline sniffed. "Now, it's Sunday. I need to get ready for church."

"Is Sunday the day your mind comes back from vacation?" Jess sneered.

"You're not too old that I won't knock you out, girl," Aveline snapped.

Jess rolled her eyes. "No offense, Momma, but I think your knocking out days are over."

Aveline looked away, wizened fingers pick at the sheets in her lap. "I wish your sister was here," she whispered.

"Well, I'm what you've got." Jess ran her fingers through her short brown hair. "Now, what do you want to wear?"

Momma was silent for a moment, breath whistling through her nose, her eyes closed for so long that for a moment, Jess thought she had fallen asleep sitting up. "Green dress, white shawl. Reverend keeps that church so damn cold, and I don't stay warm like I used to."

Jess pulled open the closet door and rifled through the few dresses and sweaters Momma had until she found the sage green dress with daisies printed on the skirt. She laid the dress out on the bed along with undergarments taken out of Momma's dresser. The one that

Pawpaw had supposedly made for her, and carved daisies into the legs and around the adjoined mirror frame.

"What are you wearing?" Aveline asked, slowly standing so Jess could help her out of her nightgown.

"I'll find something."

Aveline grunted, sitting back down and watching Jess work the sheer hose up her wrinkled legs. "Wear one of my dresses until we find you something else. I'm sure Nancy has something down at the church store."

"It'll be fine, Momma. It doesn't really matter—"

"I know the kinds of things you wear. Those little jean shorts, and tank tops, and men's boots. Showing off to everyone," Aveline scoffed. "You are not walking into the House of God looking like a slut—"

Jess huffed in irritation. "Seriously? It's a little too fucking early for this."

"Don't cuss at me, Jessamine."

"Oh, sorry, you just called me a slut, but I apologize for cussing at you, Momma," Jess snarled. "Let's just get this over with."

"I did not call you a slut—"

"Just leave it alone, Momma. I'll wear one of your damn dresses if it'll get you off my back."

Aveline snapped her mouth shut and Jess finished dressing her in the ensuing silence. While these arguments were nothing new—all of Jess' teenage years were argument after argument—Jess had been lured into a false sense of peace since returning home. Jess didn't know if she was angry or relieved that their true interactions never changed. That her mother was still in there.

"I can make something quick before we go," Jess said, picking out a dress from her mother's closet without really looking at it.

"I'll eat at the potluck after," Aveline said, pulling her shawl tight around her shoulders. "Did you make something to bring?"

"Why would I do that?"

Aveline tutted. "Right. I forget you can't cook for shit. Unless something changed?"

Jess huffed. "No, Momma, nothing changed."

"Shame."

"Cane or walker?" Jess asked, trying not to snap back.

"Walker," Aveline softly answered.

Jess pulled the walker out from beside the nightstand and set in front of her mother. She stopped and looked at her mother. Properly looked. The dress that once fit her mother perfectly, hung loose on her thin frame. Gold glinted underneath the shawl, the small cross lying in the hollow of Aveline's throat. Freckled skin sagged and wrinkled. How could so much change in seven years?

"We all get old, Jessamine," Aveline whispered. "Even me."

It's too fast.

Jessamine looked away and cleared her throat. "I'm going to change real quick. They should be here to pick us up soon."

She flew out of that room as if her life depended on it and back up the stairs to her room. The room that hadn't changed even though her mother had. If the town hadn't changed in these years, why did her mother have to? Jess plopped down on the bed, squeezing the dress in her hands, waiting for tears to come.

They didn't.

A rumbling down the road shook the floor. Jess stood and peered out the dirty glass. Nancy's grey Cadillac de Ville slowly crawled down the dirt road to pick them up.

"Shit."

Jess shucked off her nightshirt and changed her underwear before pulling the dress over her head. Pink floral fabric brushed her knees and hugged her chest, reminding her that she was much more blessed than her mother in that department. The outline of her bra pushed through the cotton.

"Shit," she repeated, plucking at the fabric and bunching it up around her chest to hide the outline and only succeeded in inching up the hem, showing enough creamy thigh to piss off every other woman there.

The biddies would have something to say about it. She could already hear their whispers buzzing around her head like gnats that just wouldn't die no matter how many times they were swatted out of the air.

One hand dragged a brush through her shoulder length hair while the other opened the drawers of the vanity she had Celia used to share, searching for the clips she knew she had left behind and hoped Celia hadn't pilfered. She twisted strands of hair back to keep it out of her face and secured it with pink and clear butterfly clips looking very much as if she were trying to recapture her look from senior year. Jess shoved her feet into the combat boots her momma apparently hated so much and hauled ass downstairs.

"Oh, well don't you look nice, dear," Nancy said, standing on the porch with one hand on her yellow wide-brimmed hat to keep it from flying away in a sharp gust of wind.

"Sorry, it was either these or flip flops," Jess muttered, holding the door open so Momma could step onto the porch, and they could get her down the steps.

"Don't worry, hun, we'll find you something," Nancy promised, holding her arm out for Aveline to grip.

The walker was carefully packed into the trunk and Jess slid into the wide back seat beside her mother. Sun-bleached leather mixed with a faded pine tree air freshener that hung from the rear-view mirror. Betty Fisher—the bangs butcher herself and Nancy's daughter—sat behind the wheel. She smiled a wide magenta smile in the mirror.

"Good to see you, Jess," she said.

"You too, Betty."

Betty frowned. "When did you cut your hair so short, darlin'? You used to have the most beautiful long hair. I always fussed at your momma when she brought you in for a trim because I hated to cut any of it."

You didn't hate it that much.

Jess offered a tight smile. "I like it short in the summer. I sweat less."

She liked it short all the time and hated the way long hair made her head feel ten times heavier. Or how people used to touch her hair without asking her, lamenting about how long and beautiful it was much like Betty was doing now.

"Well, I suppose that does make sense," Betty continued, her voice not losing an ounce of cheerfulness. Jess never knew if it was real or fake or so fake it felt real. "Everyone will be so happy to see you. They've been talking all week about you coming home."

Jess could imagine everything said about her.

The Caddy bounced on the dirt road and Jess' stomach bounced with it, threatening to empty her already empty stomach. Most of it was nerves. She had never wanted to see these people again. Never wanted to deal with their judgment because she always knew which way it would swing.

She was the first out when the car pulled onto the stretch of road in front of the church—the small parking lot already full—and grabbed Momma's walker from the trunk. All eyes were on her as she walked beside Aveline across the hot pavement and through the open doors of the church. Faded red carpet cut between wooden pews that had long since lost their glossy sheen. Two rows faced the pulpit while groupings of pews sat in the oddly angled spaces of the additions. They would only get to see the side profile of the Reverend unless he deigned to turn his head and speak to them.

Reverend Daniels waved and pointed to the empty seats in the first pew. Jess swallowed. Great. Just what she wanted. A front row seat under Reverend Daniels' scrutiny. He pursed his lips in disappointment as he stared at Jess, though she didn't know if it was because of the outfit or because he found her wanting in general.

Probably a mix of both.

As soon as she and Momma sat down, the Reverend moved his gaze away to take in his flock as a whole. His pearly-white smile reflected the bright sun that filtered in through the open windows. Despite the slight breeze, the inside of the church was sweltering. Sweat gathered in her hairline. Jess turned her head and saw a bead of foundation streak down Nancy's face. The older woman sighed and opened her fan, wrist frantically waving the fan to generate a small breeze. Others followed suit, the sound of crinkling paper filling the church.

Reverend Daniels spoke loud enough to cover the noise, but Jess tuned him out.

She had lost interest in the word of God a long time ago, and she was even less interested now. God had never been there when she needed him. Why should she give undying faith and devotion to a god who turned his gaze away from her?

Dust motes danced on the rays of sunlight. Jess followed them around the room as they swirled around the familiar faces she had known all her life but not the face she wanted to see. Sam and his family weren't there at all. Though Sam also had a rocky relationship with

God, he still came every Sunday with his parents then he'd sneak off with Jess and a few others into the woods behind church to share the joint Ben would steal from his burnout brother's stash.

Ben sat in the second pew from the back. He raised his calloused hand when he noticed Jess looking. Beside him sat Misty, oftentimes considered the school slut just because she wore short skirts and heavy makeup, her black hair pulled back into a braid. A chubby-cheeked and green-eyed baby sat in Misty's lap, fingers clutching the yellow fabric of Misty's dress, and their lips smacking around a shiny purple teething ring. Misty raised a brow and used her baby's hand to offer a wave.

"Before we conclude today's service," —Reverend Daniels' voice boomed, recapturing Jess' attention— "I'd like to welcome home our long-lost daughter, Jessamine, who has returned home after seven long years. We sure have missed her."

Polite applause followed the announcement and Jess wished the floor would split open and swallow her.

Wicker dug into her arm and she turned to find the person behind her trying to hand her the full collection plate. Jess handed it past her mother who made a small noise and held up her purse. With a soft sigh, Jess held the collection plate with one hand and rummaged through Momma's purse with the other until she produced a crumpled ten-dollar bill and tossed it onto the pile of crisply folded bills.

Reverend Daniels waited until Nancy damn near snatched the plate away from Jess and he reached for Jess' hands. Despite the heat, his hands were cold and clammy. His eyes drifted from her hair and down her torso, resting on her thighs before finally flicking back up to meet her own. Her skin crawled.

"I know your Momma is as happy that you are home as we are," he said, hands tightening around hers as if he thought she might try to flee. "If you need anything, *anything* at all, you let us know. We are here for you. Our prayers are with you."

He waited until she nodded and muttered a meek "thanks" before letting go of her hands. She shoved her now cold hands under her thighs in case he decided to grab for them again. The Reverend had always been a creep and that hadn't changed in her absence either. Rumors had churned through the mill before but most of the adults couldn't believe such things of their Reverend and so the rumors died. Jess never knew if any of it was true, but Momma never let Jess volunteer or study at the church alone and that was damning enough for her.

Jess didn't breathe again until she was outside in the muggy air that dampened the dress and made it cling to her skin. Rivulets of sweat dripped down the nape of her neck and between her shoulder blades. She pressed her hand to the space between her chest and stomach and dragged in a breath through her nose.

After church, the congregation moved to the picnic area beside the church and the thrift store. A smattering of picnic tables sat underneath sprawling willow trees, leaves dripping into the wood below. Never enough seating for everyone, but most assumed that the adults and elders would sit while the kids would run off and play after eating. Two side by side outdoor tables were set up beside the thrift store and covered in a thin plastic tablecloth bought from the dollar store a town over. The cloth was covered in faded pastel eggs. A holdover from an Easter celebration she wasn't here for.

"Why is it so damn hot?" Aveline grumbled, the wheels of her walker snagging on the uneven grass.

"It's June, Momma, and you're wearing a shawl."

Aveline tutted. "I know that, Jessamine. Help me under that shade before I melt."

Aveline sat on the edge of a bench with an exhale and leaned her elbow on the wood. "Feels like I damn near ran a race," she mumbled. "Do you have my fan, Jessamine?"

"No, I didn't grab it before we left."

Aveline cut her eyes at Jess. "I suppose you just want me to melt then?" she snapped. "Take my purse and run over to the store and get me one," —her mouth pinched as her eyes traveled down— "and pick out a nice church dress and shoes. Lord knows where you got such a dress."

Jess rolled her eyes. "It's your dress, Momma, remember?"

Aveline waved her hand. "None of my dresses look like that."

"Because you and Celia are rail thin and I'm not." Jess snatched her mother's purse, wanting to storm off, but she hesitated. "I should wait for Nancy or somebody to come sit with you."

"I'm not a child. I can handle sitting by myself for a few minutes," Aveline scoffed.

"Fine."

Jess walked past the line of women carrying out trays of food they had prepared at home and left in the church's kitchen to keep cool or warm. Husbands herded children towards the tables and waited for their wives to make them a plate. Their eyes followed Jess. Whispers she couldn't make out and didn't want to, nipped at her heels.

The bell tied around the handle of the glass door jingled as Jess pushed it open. It swung shut, trapping her inside. Alone. Finally. A moment away from judgmental stares and welcomes she didn't ask for. Next would come the prying questions. Where had she run off to? Was it worth it? Why go to college and not finish?

Jess wandered down the middle aisle, pinching the bridge of her nose and sucking in another breath.

Painted eyes of ceramic angels pricked at her back. The aisle was full of the commercially made knickknacks that the women around town went crazy for. They took road trips to other towns hunting for them or waited for the QVC specials in July and around the holidays to order the special sets. Jess poked through the shelves and even found some terrible knockoffs hidden in the back.

The door jingled.

Reverend Daniels stood on the worn welcome mat and smiled at Jess. "Just the woman I was looking for," he said, invading her space in the time it took her to blink and trapping her between him and the hard shelf. "I really am pleased your home, Jessamine. Your momma needs someone to take good care of her, and I know you'll put away the past to do that because you're a good girl."

He touched her shoulder, cold seeping through the fabric and making her shiver. Jess sank her teeth into her tongue and just nodded. The Reverend took that as a signal to grip her other shoulder and run his hands down to her upper arms.

"If you ever need someone to talk to, someone to pray with or for you, or some guidance. You only need to call or come to the church. I'm here for you," he whispered, gently squeezing her arms.

Her stomach rolled and her ears began to ring. She curled her fingers into the hem of the skirt while her hands trembled. Not because she was afraid but because she wanted to scream at him. Tell him to stop touching her. Smash her fists into his face until fragments of his teeth tore the skin from her knuckles. She wanted to bleed him. Bleed over him. Taste it in her mouth and spit it into his face.

The door jingled.

The Reverend dropped his hands from Jess' arms as Misty walked in, baby on her hip, her eyes darting around until they landed on Jess.

"I was wondering where you had run off to before I could say hi," Misty said, warmth in her gaze cooling when it landed on the Reverend. "James is asking for you, Reverend, says he wants to ask you something about the youth group."

"Ah, well I suppose I better find him then." Reverend Daniels inclined his head to Jess. "You remember what I said now, Jessamine. I'm always here for you."

Misty waited until the Reverend left the shop before rolling her eyes and huffing. "God, he's still such a creep. He was practically frothing at the mouth to get you alone."

Jess crossed her arms over her stomach. "Well, he got what he wanted."

"Good thing I came when I did," Misty said, pursing her lips. "Though you looked ready to swing. Maybe I shouldn't have."

"No, you should've. Can't imagine what would've happened if I clocked the Reverend."

Misty giggled. "I wouldn't mind finding out. Just to see the look on those old biddies' faces."

Jess grinned and shook her head. "So...you had a baby."

"Shocking, I know." Misty shifted the babbling child back up onto her hip. "And I even got married, in case you feel like keeling over now."

"To Ben."

"Yup."

Jess moved towards the counter and hoisted herself up. "How did that one happen?"

Misty shrugged. "He was a mess when Celia broke up with him and ditched town shortly after you did. We were already friends, and things just...happened after a while. He's good to me. Always has been."

"That's great, really," Jess said. "What's her name?"

"Maybe I named her Jess."

Laughter burst forth. "No, the fuck you didn't."

Misty giggled and then sobered. "No, I didn't. I named her Daisy. They were my momma's favorite flower you know."

"How is your momma?"

"Dead."

Jess winced. "Sorry."

"It's whatever, you know? I knew it was going to happen sooner or later." Misty rested her cheek on top of Daisy's head. "They found her by an empty bottle. I suppose she would've been happy to know she finished it before she choked on her own vomit."

Jess didn't know what to say.

"She wasn't the best, but she was still my mother, you know?"

Jess nodded.

Misty straightened. "Anyway, how about you? How are you holding up with...?"

"I mean," —Jess blew out a breath— "most of the time she doesn't know who I am. Today she knew me and we started arguing just like we used to. I don't know how I feel about it."

"It can't be easy, I imagine."

"Nothing about anything has been easy."

"I suppose that's why you're home and Celia isn't."

"Celia has kids and shit. I don't." Jess gently swung her legs. "I got the short end of the stick."

"Well, I am glad you're back," Misty said. "You're one of the few friends I had, and Ben and I are happy to help or hang out when we can."

Jess picked at the peeling laminate countertop. "And Sam? Do y'all still hang out?"

"Um," —Misty shifted uncomfortably— "yeah, we hang out sometimes."

Jess narrowed her eyes. "What is that?"

"What is what?"

"Every time I ask about Sam, people start acting weird."

Misty cleared her throat. "Well, it's just that...it's been a long time and things change and—"

"Has something happened? Something terrible?" Jess' voice climbed an octave with each word. "Is that it? I left and something awful happened to Sam?"

"No, no, that's not it," Misty quickly reassured her. "But you should really hear it from Sam. I don't think it would be right of me to tell you."

"I don't think Sam is going to tell me anything," Jess whispered.

Misty sighed. "I'm sorry, Jess. I'm sure there'll be an opportunity for you two to speak soon."

"If you say so."

"Listen, you ran away from this place and I fucking don't blame you. I wish I had done the same. Do you really think Sam won't understand? Or are you punishing yourself because you think it's what you deserve?"

"Fuck, Misty, I don't..." Jess' shoulders sagged. "I don't know. Maybe."

"Here," —Misty moved closer— "Ben and I got you a little something. A welcome home gift. It's in my pocket."

Jess leaned down and reached into the shallow pocket of Misty's butter yellow sun dress, pinching a plastic baggie between her fingers and pulling it out. "Really?" She waved the baggie with two impeccably wrapped joints inside. "Weed?"

"It might take the edge off," Misty said. "I'd offer to smoke it with you, but Ben and I agreed to hold off for a while. Gotta prioritize and all that."

Jess rolled her eyes with a grin and stuffed the baggie into her bra. "Thanks, I think."

Chapter 3

SAM BALANCED ON THE rickety stool behind the counter and flipped through the appointment book, pausing every so often to shove a hot Cheeto into her mouth and lick the orange dust from her fingers. Wisps of dirty blond hair escaped her ponytail and tickled her powdered cheeks. She raised a can to her lips, bubbles of Cheerwine bursting on her tongue.

The door opened letting in the sound of the high-powered drill and the smell of machine oil.

"What's up, Ben. The truck acting up again?" Sam asked. "You didn't have to bring it in, I could've swung by after the shop closed."

Ben ran his fingers through his thick dark hair. Blue eyes darted around the room. "No, the car's fine. Just wanted to pop in and see how you're doing."

Sam raised a perfectly plucked eyebrow. "Okay...I'm doing fine, Ben, how are you?"

Ben nodded, leaning his elbows on the counter and drumming his fingers on the wood. "I'm doing pretty good." He paused, looking past Sam to the calendar on the wall. "You know, uh, Jess is back in town, right?"

Of course Sam knew. Everyone was talking about it. Even though barely anyone talked to Sam anymore, she still heard things. Nancy and her ilk couldn't whisper worth a damn. Not to mention they always threw looks Sam's way whenever they mentioned Jess.

Does she know about me already?

Sam sipped her soda.

Does it disgust her?

Sam finally shrugged. "Yeah, I know."

"Yeah, yeah, cool." Ben sucked his teeth awkwardly. "So...are you going to go see her?"

"I doubt she wants to see me."

A rag smacked into the back of Sam's head and she nearly spat out her drink. Keith—Sam's father and a bear of a man—stood in the open doorway of the manager's office, *his* office, and frowned at Sam. Oil stains, both old and new, covered his faded blue jumpsuit that was zipped all the way up to his chin. The red outlined patch bore the name of Roddy's Repair in blocky blue letters on his chest. A business bought from the previous owner that only still flourished because there was no other mechanic that wasn't an hour away.

They didn't want a tranny in their church or in their grocery stores, but they had no choice but to let one work on their cars. A fact that brought Sam some amount of petty glee, though it never quite filled the hole of having her entire community ripped out from under her just because she wanted to live her life in a way that made her happy and whole.

"Not this shit again," Keith grumbled. "Letting that girl go was the stupidest thing you ever did."

Sam huffed. "She wanted to leave."

"Ain't none of us stop you from goin' with her."

Sam pursed her lips.

Ben grinned and knocked on the counter. "Does it help that she was asking Misty about you after church?"

The barest hint of butterflies broke free from their cocoons before Sam squashed them back down into goo. Seven years was a long time. Enough time for change. For feelings to die. Jess probably wasn't the same woman. Maybe she was married now. Or had a boyfriend.

Or maybe she'll hate you like everyone else.

Sam cleared her throat. "Not really. I'm sure she's just curious about what's happened to everyone while she was gone."

Both Ben and Keith sighed and shared an annoyed look.

"I don't know. She seemed pretty freaked out when she thought something bad might've happened to you." Ben shrugged. "Sure seemed more than just curiosity to me."

"What did you tell ger?" Sam asked.

"Nothing. Misty told her it should come from you, and no one else has told her as far as I know," Ben answered.

Sam snorted. "Of fucking course, any other time they can't keep business to themselves, but *this* they shut their mouths about."

"Better that way," Keith said. "You should be the one to tell her, not them twisting everything to benefit themselves."

"So, what do I do? Just call her. 'Hey Jess, it's Sam, your old boyfriend remember? Well—surprise!—I'm actually a woman.' I'm sure that'll go great." Sam tapped the silver hoop in her nostril. "What if she fucking hates me? Or thinks that I lied to her? Or trapped her?"

Keith crossed his arms over his barrel chest. "Are we remembering the same girl?"

"Maybe she's different."

Ben opened his mouth but the phone rang. Sam quickly grabbed it, thankful for the interruption before they could start up again and convince him to call her right there and then. Rip off the bandaid and all that.

"Roddy's Repair, this is Sam speaking, how may I help you?" Sam chirped with false cheerfulness.

"Hey, Sam, is Ben there?" Misty's voice came through high-pitched and with an edge that belied her patience was wearing thin while a baby cried in the background.

"Uh, yeah, he's here," Sam answered, giving Ben a look that said, "you're fucked," and Ben winced.

"Well, you tell him that his daughter is screaming like a damn harpy, and he better get his ass home with those drops that I sent him to the store over half an hour ago," Misty hollered into the phone so loud that Sam held the phone away from ear and still heard everything clearly.

Ben swallowed, backing away towards the front door. "I'm, uh, I'll see y'all later then."

"He's leaving now, Misty," Sam promised.

Misty huffed. "This colic shit is gonna kill me; I swear."

"Tell her to do that leg thing," Keith barked over his shoulder, walking back into his office.

"I've tried that," Misty grumbled.

"I'm sorry. I hope it gets better soon," Sam said.

"Why did Ben even stop by?"

"To tell me that Jess was asking about me and to try to convince me to call her."

Misty snorted. "Well you better get your shit together and do it before one of these losers try to get at her. The Reverend's son and his friends were sniffing around."

Sam scoffed. "Jess would never go for James."

"She's vulnerable now and James would absolutely take advantage of that."

"Are you suggesting I should take advantage instead?" Sam rapped her fingers on her thigh. "I'm not going to do that regardless of..."

What I still feel for her.

"What I'm saying *is*," —Misty drew out the word— "she needs someone to be there for her. A real friend. Not someone just trying to get in her pants. And maybe something more still exists between you and maybe there's nothing, but what's wrong with being friends? I—"

A screen door screeched open and clanged shut.

"Oh look, my husband is home," Misty muttered.

Sam chuckled. "Go easy on him."

"I make no promises."

"Bye, Misty."

"Think about what I said, Sam." Misty hung up.

Sam let the receiver drop into the cradle and sighed, brushing flyaway hairs from her face. Everyone had a point though she didn't want to admit it. Jess hadn't just been Sam's girlfriend, but their relationship felt deep even then. They were best friends. Confidantes. Sam wanted nothing more than to be that again.

Will that be enough?

There had been a time when Sam thought she and Jess would run off together and get married. Live the rest of their lives together. Sam had even started saving up for a ring, working extra shifts in the shop and even taking odd jobs. Then Jess had showed up that night, eyes red and puffy and devoid of that spark of light Sam loved so much, with a suitcase and had begged Sam to run away right then.

But Sam only had enough for one ticket.

Sam chose Jess. What was best for her. One bus ticket the hell out of here. Sam had hoped to join Jess soon. Get their plan back on track. Then the calls stopped coming. Sam had lived with the hurt for a long time. She didn't want to be hurt again.

Her leg jiggled making the wooden stool creak. She tapped her nails against the metallic soda can.

"Sam," Keith's normally gruff voice was unusually soft. "You won't be able to answer any of your questions if you don't talk to her. Maybe you can start up again or maybe you finally end things properly, but it's better than pining over someone who is right there."

"I know you're right," Sam whispered. "I just don't know if I can take it if she thinks awful things about me because of..." she trailed off gestured to herself.

Keith clapped her shoulder. "This was always you, Sam, even when you weren't quite sure of it. If anyone is going to see that, it's Jess." He cleared his throat. "Now, I promised your momma I'd go home a bit early and help her with something. Once you close up, you should come by for dinner before heading home."

Sam waved her hand. "That's okay, Pa, I have stuff at home."

"Your momma requested you home for dinner. Are you really going to make me tell her you're not coming?"

Sam swallowed hard. "I'll be there."

Keith nodded and tossed the keys to Sam. "See that you are, kiddo."

Left alone in the stark silence of the office, Sam watched the hands of the clock tick ever forward. The tick, tick, tick of the second hands grew louder, echoing in her ears and her brain, threatening to lull her to sleep. Sam waited for her final customer to come pick up their keys so she could lock up. And she tried very hard not to think of Jess. Of what she might say to Jess when they saw each other again. Of the disgust that might twist Jess' face into a mask of revulsion. The hour dragged by as Sam played every possible conversation in her head.

Finally, the door jingled, and a harried Geraldine Smith pushed through the door—her grandchildren's mouths sticky and red from the half-melted popsicles in their hands—and pushed the check across the counter in exchange for her keys. She gingerly pinched the keys between her fingers after Sam had set them onto the counter and ushered her grandchildren out the door lest she expose them to Sam for too long. As if they could catch being queer.

Sam always pretended it never bothered her, but she had grown up with these people. Knew them her entire life. And they so swiftly turned their back on her. She couldn't deny it hurt as much as it angered her.

Closing didn't take long. Sam walked through the quiet shop—everyone else had gone home for the day—to secure any cars left overnight and locked the garage. Money was tucked away in the safe until she could drive the hour to Jacksonville and make the deposit, and she locked up the office and the front desk. Her truck—a sun-bleached red Ford—was the only vehicle left in the parking lot.

Hot metal seared her thigh through her blue jumpsuit as she climbed into the front seat, and she hissed between her teeth. The cabin felt like a hundred degrees from sitting outside all day. Her father kept harassing her to get a sun visor and she kept forgetting. Sam rolled down the window before closing the door, begging for a breeze to cool the sweat beading in her hairline. She unzipped her jumpsuit and peeled off the sleeves, tying them around her waist, and tugged her white tank top free of the waistband. Sweat dampened the fabric gathered under her black bra.

No one had warned her properly of underboob sweat before she started hormones.

Sam hummed along to the Nirvana cassette she had popped in that morning, her thumbs tapping the steering wheel, while she pulled onto the main road and headed for her parent's house instead of home.

Home was a single wide trailer in the Marisville Park trailer park and mobile home neighborhood. It wasn't much but she had bought it with her own money though she rented the land it sat on. Even built a nice deck off the front door in a weekend. A perfect place to sit out in the early morning with coffee or the late afternoon with an iced tea.

Her parent's was closer to the farmlands. Tucked in the woods and only accessible by a long, winding, dirt road that allowed one vehicle going in one direction at any given time. She did her best to avoid the potholes that Keith had yet to fill in. Pebbles clinked against the wheel well. A squirrel scampered across the dirt road and disappeared up a tree. The driveway was a patch of dirt and grass worn away by tire tracks. Sam parked beside her little sister's purple VW Bug. A car no one approved of, but Lily usually got what Lily wanted, and their parents had relented when Lily promised to let Keith or Sam check out the car before she purchased it.

Hound, an aptly named Bloodhound that Sam had named when she was five and not very creative, stood up from where he snoozed on the porch and stretched before bounding down the steps as Sam hopped out of her truck. His ears flapped against the side of his head. A deep bark rumbled from his chest. A demand for pets.

"Hey, boy," Sam murmured, scratching Hound under his chin. "Been taking care of things while I'm away?"

Hound grumbled his assent and turned, tail lashing Sam's legs, to lead her onto the shaded porch. He danced at the screen door, fixing his pitiful gaze on Sam.

"Don't you let him back in this house!" Momma shouted from inside. "That damn dog already stole a biscuit off the counter."

Sam chuckled and patted Hound's head. "Sorry boy, Momma said no."

Hound huffed and slunk away back to his spot and flopped down, shooting Sam one last look of betrayal before closing his eyes. The screen door clattered shut behind Sam. The smell of fried chicken and biscuits made her stomach growl. Her mother peered around the corner and waved Sam into the kitchen.

"'Bout time you got here. Thought you tried to skip out on dinner."

Sam snorted. "And risk your wrath. I'm not interested in meeting God this early, Momma."

Juniper Williams—a short, plump woman of fifty-five years—snorted and shook her head, blond curls shot through with gray bouncing against her shoulders. A neckerchief kept most of them back away from her face while she waved a pot holder over a steaming hot casserole dish. Keith stood at the sink, the ever-dutiful pot washer, scrubbing the utensils Momma had already used while making her feast.

"What's the occasion?" Sam asked, perching on the bar stool at the island. "You save the casseroles for church and funerals."

And we don't go to church anymore.

"Well, after dinner I wanted to go visit. I'd hoped you'd take your father and I."

A sinking feeling in Sam's gut told her exactly where this was going but she still asked: "Visit who?"

"Jess, of course. I'm sure she has her hands full taking care of her momma and I want to make sure they're eating right," Juniper answered, her eyes not quite meeting Sam's. "I made chicken casserole, and I was gonna take her some biscuits and some sweet potato pie too. I doubt she's getting much time to cook."

"Lord knows that girl can't cook," Keith muttered.

Juniper swatted him with the potholder, but he smirked.

"You remember when she tried to make those cookies for the bake sale, and she used salt instead of sugar?" Keith chuckled. "'Bout made everyone retch."

Sam tried not to smile. "She also burnt up that pan trying to boil water once."

Keith howled with laughter and Juniper swatted him again, fighting back her own laugh. "Now, y'all stop that. Jess is blessed in many ways, but cooking just isn't one of them and we're not going to remind her of that."

Sam nodded. "She's damn good at standing up to people."

"And she has a mean right hook," Keith added.

Juniper cut her eyes at him.

Keith puffed out his chest and grinned. "I taught her that too."

Juniper rolled her eyes. "Teaching her how to scrap isn't nothing to be proud about Keith Williams."

"Bet me it ain't."

"You hush up and finish washing them dishes."

Keith turned back to washing the dishes, still snickering him to himself. Their families had been close even before Jess and Sam were born and raised around each other, but between Jess' departure and Aveline's sickness a rift had opened and pushed them all further apart. Sam wanted to be close again. To have someone. To have Jess be that someone.

"I know you're worried," Juniper said softly. "But she's going to find out one way or another and it's best if it comes from you."

"I know," Sam whispered.

Juniper reached across the butcher block countertop and patted Sam's hand. "If she's awful to you, I'll just have to kick her hind end until hell won't have it again."

The corner of Sam' mouth twitched. "Thanks, Momma."

Sam tried not to worry about it as they ate dinner, but the biscuits turned to sand in her mouth and the fried chicken became a stringy mess of meat that caught in her throat. Conversations flew in one ear and out the other. Lily told them all about her upcoming tryouts for the cheer team but Sam barely paid attention. It wasn't until Sam and her parents had climbed into the front seat of her truck that it really hit Sam that she was going to actually see Jess. Right now. No running. No excuses.

Yellow light spilled out of the windows into the dark front yard. The porch light was either off or had burned out. Sam waded her way through the tall grass, following her parents onto the bowing front porch, her heart thudding in her chest. She wished she had gone home and changed out of her oil-stained jumpsuit and the thin white tank top into something nicer. Manicured nails dragged through her hair, trying to push the wisps back.

Will Jess even recognize me?

Keith rapped his knuckles on the screen door. The sound of running water stopped and Sam's heart threatened to stop with it.

"Just a minute!" Jess called from the kitchen.

Sam's heart nearly leapt out of her chest. The muscle quivered in excitement, sending frantic signals to Sam's brain as if to say: "We know this voice. We missed this voice. It's her. She's back."

Sam shoved her shaking hands into her pockets as Jess crossed into the hallway looking the same as the day she left with the exception of her hair. Once long and nearly reaching her waist, Jess' hair was now cropped around her shoulders. Damp strands clung to her neck. She wore denim shorts and a faded shirt that Sam recognized as one of her old Carolina Panthers shirts that Jess had nicked when they had dated.

She still has it?

Bright yellow gloves covered Jess' hands as she tried to brush the strands of hair away with her arm. A smile broke out when she saw Juniper and Keith but the smile faltered as her eyes landed on Sam.

Sam waited for the curl of Jess' lip. For the hatred to spark in her gaze. But Jess' lips parted and her eyes widened. Sam almost saw the light bulb flicker to life in Jess' head.

"Sam?" Jess asked.

Sam raised her hand in an awkward wave. "Hey, Jess," she said, more aware than ever how much higher her voice was, and of the breathless edge as if she had run from her parent's house to Jess' instead of driving.

Jess blinked. "I..." she trailed off, eyes darting between the three of them before she shook her head and pushed open the screen door. "I'm sorry, I forgot my manners, come in."

Juniper's shoulders relaxed and she smiled. "It's so good to see you, Jess."

"Hope it's not a bad time," Keith added, clapping Sam on the back and offering a gruff smile.

They had been worried too. Sam hadn't noticed until now.

"Not all! I'm just cleaning up the kitchen." Jess waved her gloved hands apologetically as she led them into the kitchen. Dishes cluttered the counter next to the sink as if she hadn't washed them in a few days, and knowing Jess, she probably hadn't.

Juniper clicked her tongue against her teeth. "My goodness, darlin', why don't you let me help."

"Oh, that's not—"

"Nonsense," Juniper cut her off. "I'll just put this casserole in the fridge first. Open the door for me, Sam."

"Sure," Sam muttered and opened the fridge door. She blinked at the mess of casserole dishes and tupperware containers—which weren't actual tupperware containers, but everyone called their used and washed-out margarine containers tupperware.

Juniper sighed. "Oh my."

Pink crept up Jess' cheeks. "Everyone keeps sending food," she mumbled. "It's...a lot."

Sam knew what she meant. Everyone kept bringing food and false reassurances that Jess wasn't alone, but did any of them actually stay? Did they help? No. They patted themselves on the back and left Jess alone in an old house and a sick mother.

Juniper set the dish down on the table and Keith did the same with the containers he was carrying. "Let me have the gloves, hun," Juniper said to Jess, holding out her hands. "Why don't you take a moment and sit down."

"You don't—"

"No arguing, missy. I'm gonna set this kitchen back to rights," Juniper said.

No one argued with her and won.

Jess peeled off the rubber gloves and handed them to Juniper, looking more relieved than anything else. "Thank you."

"Hey, Sam, why don't you check out the car? I've been meaning to come around and take a look at it," Keith said. "Take Jess with you so she can get some fresh air."

Slick.

Sam nodded. "I need the keys."

Jess opened the junk drawer and shoved batteries and random greeting cards aside to grab the keys. She handed them to Sam, their fingers brushing for the briefest of moments. Long enough for the air to squeeze out of Sam's lungs. Could she really feel the same after all these years? How could Jess make her heart hammer in her throat from the barest of touches?

Metal screeched as Sam popped the hood to the Oldsmobile. The lack of porch light left her squinting down at the vague, dark shapes. She could've walked to her car and grabbed her flashlight, but she felt Jess' gaze boring into her face.

"You might as well ask," Sam said, looking up to meet Jess' gaze. "I know you want to."

Jess' head was tilted to the side, her arms crossed under her chest as if she were hugging herself. Did Sam make her nervous? "When?" Jess' asked, barely above a whisper. "When did you know?"

Sam shrugged. "I think a part of me always knew, but I started transitioning about two years after you left."

Jess didn't say anything at first. The silence stretched taut between them like a rubber band ready to snap. "I'm sorry I stopped call—"

"We don't have to get into that." Sam's voice was sharper than she intended.

"Sorry," Jess whispered. She leaned her hip on the side of the car. "I guess this is why you weren't at church."

"Yeah, nobody took well to...the change."

Jess hummed. "And your parents stopped going too?"

"Ma threatened to knock Nancy out because she wouldn't stop saying nasty things about me. They weren't exactly welcome after that."

Jess pressed her hand to her mouth to quell her laugh. "I would've paid to see that."

"Me too."

Sam leaned down and tapped a gasket, pretending she was doing something to keep Jess here. To keep her talking. God, Sam had missed her voice. Had missed Jess' lips pressed to her ear, whispering a joke in the middle of service and both of them trying not to laugh. The late-night conversations, phone cradled against Sam's face, as Jess' voice grew sleepy and distant until her soft breaths crackled through the receiver. Whispered affections as Jess' skin slid against hers, legs wrapped around Sam's waist.

She's not going to see me that way anymore.

Sam risked a look at Jess, but Jess was looking towards the pond, a faraway look in her eyes. Her fingers trailed over her arms, tracing absent designs. Teeth dug into her bottom lip.

"What are you thinking about?" Sam whispered.

"Hm?" Jess turned her head to face Sam. "I was just thinking back."

"To what?"

"There were these times that you'd look in the mirror," —Jess dropped her arms and shoved her hands into her pockets— "and you'd look sad. I didn't think much of it then." She sighed. "I wish I had been there for you."

"Maybe you should've called," Sam attempted to tease, but her voice was too serious.

"I thought you didn't want to get into that."

Sam sighed and straightened up. "I...I do, I'm just—I'm honestly not sure I want to know why you stopped calling."

Jess pulled her lip into her mouth and Sam knew she was tugging the skin from her lip. Part of her wanted reach for Jess. Brush her fingers over Jess' chin and gently tell her to stop.

"I wish I had some big explanation for you, but I don't." She shrugged, pushing her hair behind her ear. "Life was just not what I expected. It was easy to tell myself I would call later because I had to work or I was going out and then I just...stopped. I'm sorry."

Sam wiped her hands off on her pants. What could she say to that? Life happened and they drifted apart, and she knew that might happen when Jess left. Maybe if Sam hadn't taken so long to join her. Sam could what if herself to death.

"So..." Jess murmured, looking at the car. "What's the verdict?"

"Well, to be honest, I can't see shit in the dark."

Jess tilted her head back, laugh echoing in the dark, and Sam's chest grew warm. She wanted to hear that laugh all the time. Maybe she could.

"I could come back tomorrow after work. Take a better look," Sam offered.

"Are you sure?" Jess asked. "I don't want to take up your time, and I'm not sure what we could afford to fix. Mom's income is limited to dad's pension."

"You don't have to worry about that. Dad and I will make sure the car is fixed." Sam closed the hood. "But until then, if you need a ride or anything, you can call me. I'll leave my number, but you can also probably find me at the shop."

Jess looked down at her feet and absently kicked a piece of gravel. "That easy?"

"What do you mean?"

She looked up under her eyelashes at Sam. "I fucked up, but I can just ask for help and rides? You're not going to make me beg for forgiveness?"

"Do you want me to make you beg?" Sam asked, eyebrow raised.

Jess swallowed, red creeping up her neck. "N-no. I just thought you'd be angrier."

"Maybe I wasn't angry at all. Maybe I just missed you," Sam whispered.

Sam didn't know when they had gravitated towards each other, but Jess was so close. Dark eyes, mesmerizing even in the dark, threatened to pull Sam in. All she had to do was lean down. Close the distance a little more. Did Jess want to kiss her too?

"I missed you too," Jess murmured, tongue wetting her bottom lip. "I've wanted to see you since I got back."

"Me too."

Jess closed the distance, arms wrapping around Sam's waist and her face pressing into the skin of Sam's neck. Sam sighed in relief. All of that worry for nothing. They clicked back into place as if the last seven years didn't happen. They were still Jess and Sam.

And Sam still loved her.

Chapter 4

To say Jess was excited about seeing Sam again was an understatement. A few simple words between them and the worries she had held over reconnecting had melted away as easily as she had melted into Sam's arms. There were a few differences now to Sam's embrace. The soft breasts that she hadn't had before, the long wisps of hair that had tickled Jess' cheeks, and the blunt nails that had dragged up and down Jess' spine, sending sparks racing across Jess' skin.

She had almost kissed Sam. Had wanted to know if Sam still tasted of Cheerwine and those strawberry candies she used to nick from the Church's candy dish, shoving them into her pockets as if they couldn't buy them at the general store for less than a dollar.

Maybe they could find their way back to that.

Jess laid in bed, sheets kicked off to the side so she could welcome the gentle breeze from her window onto her sweltering skin, her forefinger dragging over her bottom lip. A soft cry crackled through the baby monitor. Jess glared balefully at the flickering green light. A cough followed the cry.

"Couldn't you sleep in, just once," she mumbled, pushing up onto her elbows and swinging her feet to the floor. Murky water splashed onto her heels and up her ankles.

Jess grunted in disgust. "What the—?"

She tilted her head up to the unblemished ceiling, searching for a stain or droplets of water but found nothing. Jess stood. Small puddles led from the window and stopped at her bed. Had it rained sometime in the night? How did the water get in this far?

Weird.

Another cough came through the baby monitor and Jess huffed. She poked her head out into the hall. "I'll be down in a minute, Momma," she called down the stairs.

She stomped from her room and into the hall bathroom, grabbing her towel from where it hung on the bar and wiped the water from her feet. *Momma first, clean up later.* Another cough echoed up the stairs. She tossed the towel to the floor and hurried into the hall before Momma hacked up a lung trying to get Jess' attention.

The door to her grandfather's room was cracked open. Jess frowned. She didn't remember opening the door and there was no way Momma could get up the stairs. The hinges squeaked as she pushed it open and looked inside.

Pawpaw was a simple man. Not that Jess really remembered him. There were times she sometimes recalled the wrinkled and graying man who used to give her ice-cold lemonade after she and Celia would spend most of the hot, muggy afternoons swimming in the pond. But he had died when she was twelve. Disappeared during a hunting trip and nobody ever found him. Momma had cried for weeks, and cried again when they held a funeral with an empty casket. All that was left was a room with nothing more than a four-poster bed with hand carved posts, a dresser, and a mirror Momma had covered with a white sheet and never taken off.

Jess pulled the door closed. Maybe she had stepped on a floorboard and the door popped open. Her closet did the same thing.

"I'm coming, Momma," she said, taking the stairs and turning down to her mother's room. "There was water on my floor and—"

Aveline sat on the side of the bed, her nightgown damp with a faint yellow stain. The acrid smell of urine made Jess wrinkle her nose. Had it happened because Jess had taken too long? Or had it happened sometime in the night? Aveline stared down at her lap in surprise as if she couldn't quite believe she had pissed herself.

What am I supposed to do?

Neither Celia nor Derotha had gone over what to do if this happened. Could Jess just put her mother in the shower? The tub didn't feel entirely safe, but Jess didn't have many options. "I'll be right back," she murmured, and ran for the safety of the kitchen.

She barely felt the weight of the cordless phone in her hands. Shrill rings trilled in her ears. She tapped her fingers against the side of the refrigerator, the dull thuds mixing with the ringing in her ears. Derotha didn't answer. Jess cursed under her breath and slammed the phone back down into the charger. Why did Celia leave her here to deal with this alone? What would've been so hard about having Momma move in with her? Or moving the kids and her husband here?

Why didn't either them plan for something like this?

Aveline still sat where Jess had left her, nightgown pulled down her shoulder as if she had tried to take off her soiled clothing and gave up.

"Let's get you in the shower, Momma," Jess said, holding her arms out to help her mother stand and get her down the hall to the bathroom.

Aveline pushed her hands away. "I don't need your help, Jessamine. I just need a moment to get my legs under me."

"Please just let me help—"

"I said I don't need your damn help!" Aveline snapped. "I'm not an invalid. I can clean myself up. Now go."

Jess pinched the bridge of her nose. "I'm not saying you can't clean yourself, but I don't want you to fall trying to get into the shower."

"I think you'd be awfully happy if I did fall, you ungrateful shit."

Blood rushed to her cheeks. Thundered in her ears. Momma had called her many things over the years, but had never cussed at her with such vitriol. Jess curled her hands into fists. Nails dug into her palms. She forced herself to breathe through her nose.

"Momma, that's enough. If you really don't want my help, I'll try calling Derotha again, but you can't stay like this," Jess forced out through clenched teeth.

"I want Celia, she—"

"Celia isn't here, I am!" Jess exploded. "I am what you have right now, and I am trying my best to help you, but you won't stop being a stubborn old woman for five fucking minutes!"

Aveline snapped her mouth shut. She glared at Jess. Seconds turned into minutes. Neither of them spoke. Jess' chest heaved. Red spots danced on the edge of her vision. She wanted to hit something. Someone. She shoved her hands in her pockets.

"Fine," Aveline finally said, looking away first.

Despite her arguments, she leaned heavily on Jess as they walked down the hall. She waited on the toilet seat while Jess turned on the shower and adjusted the water until it was warm without being hot and was silent as Jess helped her strip out of her nightgown. With her fingers digging into Jess' shoulder, Aveline lowered herself onto the porcelain bottom of the tub and let the water wash over her.

"Will you be okay while I strip your bed?" Jess asked, handing her a washcloth.

Aveline nodded.

Jess carried the nightgown and sheets through the back door in the kitchen and into the laundry room set off the back porch. A dingy, unfinished room with just enough space for the ancient washing machine and the lawn mower that Jess didn't think worked anymore. The washing machine rattled as she turned it on and it filled with water. She watched the agitator spin, small tears trickling down her cheeks and splashing into the frothy water. The lid slammed shut with a metallic clang.

"Better?" she asked, walking back into the bathroom, her face free and clear of any tears.

"I'm sorry," Aveline murmured, unfocused eyes staring at the drain. "I didn't mean it."

"It's fine, Momma."

As luck would have it, Derotha called back after Jess had made breakfast, given Momma her medicine, and settled her down in front of the television with the morning news.

"I'm so sorry, hun," Derotha said. "We've been waiting on your Momma's insurance to approve a shower chair, but you know how those companies are. They like taking folks' money but never want to pay out money."

"It's fine." Jess scooped coffee grounds into the pot. "We figured it out this morning."

"Did she have an incident?"

Jess closed the lid and flipped the switch. "Yes, does she have them often?"

"A few times, but I wouldn't call that often. Lord knows, trying to get her to wear those undergarments is damn near impossible." Derotha sighed. "But this is a lot even for her. The times she's present take their toll too."

Jess rested her hip against the counter. "Our arguments are sometimes worse than they've ever been."

"Personality changes are very common with this illness. There are times you might not recognize her at all, but underneath, she is still there and she just can't help it."

"Is it going to get worse?" Jess whispered.

"It may. Some forms of dementia are more aggressive than others. She may plateau and then get worse or she may stay at this level, it's so hard to tell with some patients, and your Momma has always been a fighter."

Jess sighed, running her fingers through her hair. "I hope it doesn't."

"Me too." There was a soft rustling sound as Derotha switched the phone to her other ear. "Would you like me to stop by today? I'll be done with my last patient by four today and I can swing by."

Jess peeked into the living room where Momma silently watched TV, her fingers scratching the arms of the recliner. "I think we'll be fine until tomorrow."

"Alright, darlin'. I'll see you then."

The shaking in the back of the house stopped before Jess poured her cup of coffee.

"I'm going to hang up the laundry; I'll be right back," Jess said but her mother didn't respond.

Her shirt grew damp from the sheets pressed to her front. The fabric stretched over the old line making it sag in the middle. Grass tickled the edges of the sheet. A line that needed replacing. Grass that needed mowing. Problem after problem mounting up. A growing list that Jess wasn't sure she could ever complete on her own. She wheeled the lawnmower out of the back room and around to the front yard so she could take a look at it after she cleaned up the mysterious puddle in her room.

Coffee sat forgotten in the pot as Jess kept herself busy, going from room to room and opening the windows to air out the house—especially in Momma's room—and cleaning up what was left of the brackish water that stained her floor. She shoved the dirty towels in the hamper with the rest of her clothes. Balancing the basket on her hip while she stepped out of the bathroom, she noticed Pawpaw's door was open again.

With a frown, she pulled the door closed.

The sheets were in a heap on the ground, the line snapping just like she hoped it wouldn't. Jess huffed. She tossed the basket onto the cement floor by the washer and stomped to the line. Beetles flew, clicking loudly, as she shook the sheets and carried them to the front porch to lay them over the railings. She searched the back room for spare cord but found nothing.

"Shit." She smacked the top of the washer.

Jess finally poured her cup of coffee while dialing the number for the mechanic's shop.

"Roddy's Repair, this is Sam speaking, how can I help you?"

Jess' heart picked up, thumping in her ears. "Hey, it's me."

The line was silent for a moment and Jess worried that Sam hadn't meant any of what she said. That she was actually going to punish Jess.

"Hey," Sam said, voice soft and almost shy. "What's up?"

Jess picked at a loose string on her shorts. "I was wondering if I could ask a favor? If you were still planning on coming by, that is."

"I was. What do you need?"

"The line broke outside and I can't find any replacement. I was wondering if you had some."

"Uh, yeah, I can bring some..." Sam trailed off and Jess heard muted whispering in the background.

"I'm sorry, I shouldn't have called now. I'm sure you're busy—"

"No, no, it's fine," Sam reassured her. "I-I'm glad you called, really. Do you need me to bring anything else?"

Jess took a sip of her coffee and grimaced at the bitterness. Needed more sugar. "A new life," she muttered.

"Bad day?"

"Just a rough start." She sighed and leaned back in the dining chair. "I swear I barely get any sleep most days. I think about napping but…"

"You're worried something will happen?" Sam guessed.

"Yeah."

"Something might happen. Could happen anytime really even if you're watching her like a hawk."

"Well, that's not all that reassuring."

Sam snorted. "What I mean is, sometimes things happen and there's nothing we can really do about it. You're there. You're doing your best. That's all you can do really."

"How do you know I'm doing my best?" Jess questioned, looking up at the peeling popcorn ceiling.

"Because you always do even when you don't want to. You can't help it," Sam teased. "And because I know, even with everything that's gone on between you and your momma, you still love her."

Jess pressed her lips together. "Maybe I've changed."

"You probably have to some degree, but I don't think *that* has changed about you."

Jess turned in her chair to look at her mother. "You might be a little right."

Sam chuckled. "I thought so. I—"

Keith's voice barked something unintelligible in the background.

"Listen, I got to go, but I'm off a bit early today. I'll bring the cord for the clothing line when I come look at the car, okay?"

"I'll see you then," Jess said, sighing heavily as the line went dead. She wished they could have talked longer. They used to talk for hours on the phone. Even when they ran out of things to say, sometimes they would just sit there in silence with each other.

Jess drained the dregs of her coffee and put the cup in the sink. While there was an endless amount of chores to do, Jess wanted just a little bit of rest. She turned back to the living room and jumped. Momma stood at the bottom of the stairs; her gaze affixed to Pawpaw's open door.

"Momma?"

Aveline didn't look at her. Didn't even appear to have heard Jess speak to her. Her eyes were wide. Mouth set in a grim line. If Jess didn't know better, she'd think her mother looked afraid.

Jess touched her shoulder. "Mo—"

"He won't like it, Lottie," Aveline whispered. "If he finds out he...he..."

"Momma," Jess raised her voice and Aveline's gaze snapped to hers, pupils blown wide. "Momma, it's me, Jess."

Aveline dragged in a shuddering breath. "Oh, Jessamine." She looked back up the stairs. "What were we talking about?"

"We weren't, Momma." Jess gently led her back to her chair. "Had you fallen asleep?"

"I—possibly, yes," Aveline muttered.

Jess sat on the edge of the couch. "Who's Lottie?"

"Who?"

"You said the name Lottie."

Aveline's eyebrows knit together. "I don't know. I don't think..." she trailed off, eyes moving to the TV. "The weatherman was talking about a hurricane. We should check the supplies."

Jess huffed and sat back on the couch. "Great. Just what I need to worry about."

Momma didn't say anything else about hurricanes or someone named Lottie. Maybe she had misremembered someone but...

Why had she looked so afraid?

Jess stretched out on the couch and watched the washed-out visage of the weatherman pointing to a swirling mass of clouds far out in the Atlantic. The cone of uncertainty pointed the storm in the general direction of the Carolina coast but nothing that indicated it would for sure hit anywhere close by. Jess could only hope that fucker turned upward and dissipated in the cold water. A disappointment for all hurricane kind. The droning of the weatherman and the cloying heat lured her into the worst kind of sleep.

She couldn't move or speak but she was aware of everything. The weatherman disappearing in favor of a soap opera that Jess never remembered the name of. The soft breaths of her mother sat still in the recliner. The whisper of the curtains in the breeze.

An incessant dripping.

Jess didn't know where it was coming from in the house. Was it where the water on her floor had come from? It sounded close but yet far. She wanted to get up and search for it, but she couldn't make herself open her eyes.

A low rumbling came down the road and stopped in front of her house. She knew it was Sam before she even heard the squeak of hinges that needed oiled and the thump of work boots on the porch. Sam knocked and then the screen door inched open.

"Poor thing is exhausted," Aveline whispered.

"So I heard," Sam whispered back. "How are you, Miss Aveline?"

"I've been better, and I've certainly been worse." The recliner creaked. "I'm glad you're here, Sam."

"Oh?"

"She's gonna need you," Aveline said.

"I don't know about that."

"I do. One of the perks of being old. I know these things." Aveline chuckled. "How are you doing, Sam?"

"The same as you are, I guess."

"Don't pay these people no mind. Close-minded peckerheads—"

Sam coughed a laugh.

"They spend all week sinning and then pray for forgiveness on Sunday. A church full of hypocrites."

"Then why do you still make me take you?" Jess finally managed to mumble through the hazy hold of exhaustion.

"I don't go for them, Jessamine."

Jess cracked open her eyes and blinked at them both. Sam knelt in front of the couch wearing a similar jumpsuit as she had the night before, but this one was black and the sleeves were tied around her waist. A black crop top clung to Sam's soft belly. Jess swallowed, reminding herself that her mother was right beside them. Sam held up a skein of cord tied around itself to hold it together.

"Thanks," Jess said, and slowly pushed herself up onto her elbows. "Now I can finish laundry."

Sam smiled, glossy lips tempting Jess to inch closer. "Exciting," she teased.

Jess snorted. "Laundry is the farthest thing from exciting."

"Will you be staying for dinner, Sam?" Aveline interrupted.

Sam rubbed the back of her neck. "Oh, um..."

"You can, if you want," Jess said before Sam could decline. "I was just going to heat up the casserole your mom brought."

Sam's smile made Jess' heart soar. "Sure. That sounds good."

"Thank goodness," Aveline muttered as Sam grabbed the keys and retreated outside. "Thought I was going to have to guilt her into staying."

"Why?"

Aveline cut her eyes at her daughter. "Because leaving her behind was the most foolish thing you've ever done. Don't let her get away again."

Jess huffed and stood up. "It's not like that anymore, Momma."

"Bullshit." Aveline wagged her finger at her. "Mark my words, Jessamine. Don't make the same mistake twice."

Sam was under the hood of the car, muscles flexing as she unscrewed something on the engine or battery or whatever the fuck lived under the hood of a car—Jess didn't know shit about them. All she could stare at was the sweat carving trails down Sam's muscular back and the belly that peeked out from below the hem of her crop top. Jess tightly gripped the cord in her hands. Christ, she should've gone out back and taken care of the line first because now she had no intentions of walking away from watching Sam work.

"What's with the lawnmower?" Sam asked, turning her head to affix her bright blue eyes on Jess.

"I brought it out to look at it. Maybe try to tackle some of this yard soon." Jess tore her eyes away before she melted into a puddle. "My legs itch every time I look at the grass."

Sam pushed herself away from the car and Jess swore there was a swagger in her step as she knelt by the lawnmower. Her fingers curled around the handle and she lifted it up to look under it. "Well...there's no blades on it so I don't think you're going to be cutting anything anytime soon."

Jess huffed. "Of course there aren't."

Sam unscrewed a few caps and hummed under her breath. "No oil or gas either. I'm gonna guess the spark plugs are possibility burnt out too." She replaced the caps and stood up, brushing her hands on her jumpsuit. "I'm not great at small engine repair but one of the guys at the shop is. I can take it in to him, though it might be a bit before it's ready."

Jess ran her fingers through her hair. "So, long grass it is, I guess."

Sam cut her a sideways glance. "I could borrow dad's riding mower and haul it over this weekend. Will take quick care it."

"You're gonna fix my mower, my car, and mow my grass?" Jess gently nudged Sam with her elbow. "Anything else you're planning on doing?"

Sam smirked and looked back at the porch. "Your porch could use some work."

"Oh lord, you'll be here forever if you start fixing up the house," Jess teased.

"That wouldn't be so bad."

Her skin buzzed with electricity at the seriousness of Sam's tone. If Sam wanted to come over damn near every day, Jess wouldn't stop her.

"I didn't realize you had moved from mechanics to carpentry," Jess said instead of what she really wanted to say. Something along the lines of: "Please don't leave. Ever."

Sam shrugged. "I like working with my hands. Which confused a lot of folks when I told them I was a woman."

"Naturally, if you're going to commit to being a woman you might as well shove yourself into the embittered housewife mold," Jess scoffed and sat down on the porch steps, wiping sweat from her warm brow.

Sam sat down beside her. "Our favorite mold."

Jess snickered.

Sam pressed her shoulder to Jess'. "What about you?"

"What about me?"

"What do you like doing now? What did you do while you were gone?"

Jess stared down at her bare feet digging into the ground. "I worked at first. Started out as a waitress and then one night our bartender called out, so I got a crash course, realized bartenders made good tips, and started doing that. Took some day classes at the local community college and then transferred to a four year a few towns away when I got my Associate's. Worked and went to school while living in an off-campus apartment with some roommates."

Sam nodded along. "That only answers one of my questions."

"Does it?"

"You didn't sound as if you liked any of that."

Jess shrugged. "I liked some things. Think I liked bartending the best. Met some cool people. And college was nice in some respects. I liked some of the classes, but I think I liked the partying a little more, and a little too much honestly."

"What were you studying?"

Jess blew out a breath. If anyone else were asking, she would give bullshit answers to get them off her back. "I couldn't decide. I kept changing majors but never really settled on anything. And then I just..."

Stopped going. Didn't leave my apartment for anything.

"Maybe it wasn't for you then," Sam said softly. "College isn't the end all, be all."

Jess plucked a long strand of grass and twisted it around her finger. "It pisses me off that everyone was right."

"Right about what?"

"That I'd fail out there. That I'm not good at anything."

"Nobody worth anything thought you would fail," Sam said. "And you are good at things."

"Like what?" Jess scoffed.

"You're creative. I remember reading those poems and stories you used to write in math class, and your sketchbook from art class. I might even still have some stashed away somewhere."

Jess rolled her eyes. "Not exactly something I can make a living out of." She tossed the braided piece of grass into the yard. "Besides, I don't do any of those things anymore."

"Why not?"

Jess leaned back on her elbows. "There's just...nothing there anymore."

Sam pursed her lips. "Maybe you can find it again."

"Maybe."

Sam patted the top of Jess' hand and Jess sucked in a breath. "There's plenty of time to figure it out, Jess."

I'm not so sure anymore.

Chapter 5

JESS BLINKED IN THE darkness, unsure of what woke her from a dream she couldn't remember. The room was still and silent. No wind blew through the cracked open window. She couldn't even hear the sound of cicadas screaming from their perches. Her eyes strayed to the baby monitor on her nightstand. All she heard was Momma's gentle breathing through the speaker. Jess laid back down, pulling the thin sheet to her chin and curling up on her side, waiting for sleep to take her again.

Drip, drip, drip.

Jess' eyes shot back open. She had heard the same sound while napping that day on the couch. Leaning over, she looked down at the floor, but it was dry. She looked up at the ceiling—also, dry.

Shoving off the sheets, she stood and pulled the hem of her oversized shirt out of the waistband of her underwear. Jess stepped out into the hall and listened for the sound again, twisting her head back and forth, but the dripping had stopped. Maybe she had imagined it. Perhaps it was lack of restful sleep playing a trick on her mind. She turned to go back to bed.

Drip, drip, drip.

Jess' head snapped to the side. The sound was closer than before. Clearer. The bathroom maybe. Jess pushed open the door and listened, hoping it was nothing more than a leaky faucet. That would be an easier fix than an issue with the pipes in the walls or water damage coming in from the roof.

Nothing.

Jess huffed.

She walked around the hall, the darkness hazy around the edges. Shadows warped along the wood paneling covering the bottom half of the wall. Tendrils snaked over the peeling wallpaper, the floral pattern long since faded. Jess swallowed.

It's just darkness. Nothing scary.

Pawpaw's door clicked and slowly swung open. Jess' heart stuttered.

Drip, drip, drip.

Her feet carried her forward though her brain screamed for her to stop. There was something in there. Watching her. She felt the burning gaze of eyes boring into her chest. But she couldn't stop herself from pushing the door open the rest of the way. Something stirred deep in her stomach. A rumbling. An emptiness. A *hunger*. It didn't come from her, but she felt it so hard her gut ached.

A shadow unfurled from the bed. No eyes but she felt its gaze. The twist in her gut was replaced with warmth. Glee. Giddiness. As if the shadow was happy she was here. Back home where she belonged. Close enough for its gaping maw to close over her and trap her.

Jess couldn't move. Couldn't run as the shadows reached for her. Cold brushed over her skin. Pushed its way into her mouth and iced its way down her throat. Jess whimpered, unable to even muster a proper scream.

A pounding resounded in her head, growing louder and louder and—

Jess woke with a gasp.

She stood in Pawpaw's room, facing the dusty bed, with her arms tensed at her sides—so much so that they ached—and her hands clenched into fists. Wobbly knees gave out and Jess hit the floor. She sucked in shaky breaths. Tears gathered in her eyes. Her heart quivered erratically in her chest and pulsed in her neck, feeling very much as if she were having a heart attack.

The pounding stopped and she absently registered that someone was at the front door. She couldn't make herself move. Couldn't go down the stairs and answer the door. She was frozen. Chest heaving. The flimsy muscle of her heart threatening to give out. The room grew hazy. Black spots danced on the edges. Jess couldn't catch her breath, each one wheezing in and out of her but didn't reach her lungs.

Calloused fingers grasped hers. One pressed her fingers to the steady beat of a pulse under soft skin and the other held her hand against a soft chest, slowly inflating and then deflating. Dry lips rested against her temple.

"Breathe in," Sam murmured.

Jess focused on the rise of the chest under her fingers and tried to mimic, breath still stuttering in time with her heart.

"Slow," Sam drew out the word. "In and out, baby. You can do that, okay?"

Jess nodded. She didn't know how much time passed before she finally breathed in time with Sam. Awareness slowly crept back in. She had been sleepwalking again. Something she hadn't done in a long time. Not since she left home all those years ago. Even after the things that happened while she was away, she never sleepwalked.

"How did you get in?" she finally mumbled, her cheek pressed against Sam' chest instead of her hand. She listened to the gentle thump of Sam's heart.

"Momma has a key. We got worried when you didn't answer."

"They're here."

"Pop wanted to come help with the mowing and Momma came to take over your kitchen."

"Momma." Jess suddenly remembered she should've been woken by Momma's coughing through the baby monitor.

"Don't worry, Momma's handled that," Sam reassured, rubbing Jess' back. "Just take a moment and keep breathing."

Jess' eyes fluttered closed and she let herself be held. She tried not to think about the dream and how it had led her into Pawpaw's room.

"When did you start sleepwalking again?" Sam asked.

"Just now."

"Any particular reason?"

"Probably just the stress," Jess mumbled.

She used to sleepwalk all the time in her adolescent years. Most of the time she stayed in the house but there were times Celia or Momma would find her in the backyard or on the back porch. They constantly worried Jess would walk into the pond and drown before waking up. Sam snuck over many nights and squeezed herself into Jess' bed to keep Jess from going far *if* she managed to climb over Sam without waking her.

Sam brushed hair away from Jess' face. "You'll tell me if it gets worse?"

"Yes."

Jess didn't know if she would. She didn't want to worry Sam. And she didn't want Sam to tell Celia just in case Celia freaked out and tried to have Jess admitted again. It was bad enough Jess wasn't taking the pills the doctors had prescribed. She left the brown bottle sitting in the bottom of her duffel bag and kicked it under her bed. She didn't want them. Didn't like how groggy they made her feel. And they didn't do shit for the anxiety like the doctors promised her.

Sam's lips brushed over her forehead so light that Jess wasn't sure the gesture was real for a moment. "Momma brought breakfast for you if you're ready to eat."

"Okay."

They didn't go right downstairs. Jess took a moment for herself in the bathroom and freshened up, changing into shorts and a tank top with her bathing suit underneath. She needed to go outside. Do something with her hands. Feel the sunlight on her skin to chase away the vestiges of shadow that clung to her mind from the dream. And after all that working and sweating, she fully intended to jump into the pond to cool off.

Having the Williams here was a relief. She didn't have to go through the day alone with Momma. Didn't have to deal with the constant silence save for the whirring of fans and whatever they were watching on TV.

Juniper Williams gently ruffled Jess' hair while Jess scarfed down the pancakes loaded with butter and syrup, and sausage links she dragged through the leftover syrup. "Rough night?" Juniper asked.

Jess nodded with a mouthful of pancake and washed it down with a sip of coffee. "Weird dreams. Not getting much sleep as it is."

"No, I imagine you're not. I'm sure you're always listening out for your Momma."

Jess sucked down the rest of her coffee and carried her dirty dishes to the sink. "I'm always worried something is going to happen when I'm not paying attention."

Juniper patted her cheek. "Why don't you go get some fresh air while I keep an eye on things in here."

"What are you going to do?"

"Well, thought you might like a family meal and since you can't come to us, we came to you."

"Thank you," Jess murmured. "I really appreciate you being here."

"We're family, hunny, no matter what," Juniper promised.

Jess paused on her way out the kitchen. "Could you teach me how to cook?"

Juniper raised an eyebrow. "Why now?"

"I'd like to be able to cook something decent, for Momma and myself."

Maybe I won't have to rely so much on everyone else dropping off more food than we can handle.

"You let me know when you're ready, and I'll teach you what I can." Juniper turned back to washing the breakfast dishes, humming a soft tune under her breath. A lullaby Jess recognized as the one Momma used to sing to her when she had nightmares.

Warm sun was a balm on her clammy skin. Jess tilted her face up to greet the harsh yellow rays, heralded by the screeching of cicadas fluttering their wings on trees. Sweat slicked her skin nearly instantly. Fabric clung to her torso and she couldn't wait to fling herself into the pond later and wash the film from her body.

"Better?" Sam asked, fingers brushing Jess' wrist as if she wanted to hold her hand.

Jess nodded.

"You ever been on a riding mower, Jess?" Keith hollered from across the yard, standing next to a vivid green mower and waving for her to come over.

"Oh good, now he can talk your ear off about how much he loves that thing," Sam snorted.

Jess stifled a laugh. "That bad?"

"Do not ask him any questions if you want to get away anytime soon."

Jess patiently listened to Keith's presentation of the mower and all its features, climbing on when he was finished speaking, and letting him turn it on for her. She was suddenly thankful that her old push mower didn't work. There was something...fun about driving the monstrosity around the yard and cutting the grass down to size. Enough for the bugs to still have their home, but Jess wouldn't itch so much as she tried to trek through it. Keith took over halfway while Sam used the weed whacker close to the house.

"About time for lunch," Juniper said, stepping onto the porch with the cordless phone in her hand. "My goodness, you have a yard."

Jess stood, a handful of weeds in her hand, and grinned. "Imagine that."

Momma's garden had long since been choked out by dandelions and creeping sweet grass. Daffodils and daisies smothered by sticky, tangled vines that pricked at Jess' fingers as she ripped them free of the dank soil.

"Celia is on the phone," Juniper said, holding up the cordless.

The bundle of weeds fell to the ground with a soft plop. Jess brushed the crumbs of dirt onto her shorts and grasped the warm plastic. Despite the warmth seeping through her clothes, Jess felt a chill creep up her spine. What if they had called Celia and told her about Jess' episode? She swallowed, fitting the receiver between her ear and her shoulder.

"What's up?" she said in an effort to keep her voice nonchalant. No need to tip off Celia just in case no one told her anything.

"Miss Juniper answering the phone was a pleasant surprise," Celia chirped and Jess' shoulders relaxed. "I take it you took my advice and called Sam?"

"Not really. She sort of showed up on my doorstep with a casserole."

"Oh, good, at least I know Momma is eating well."

Jess rolled her eyes. "Yes, yes, my cooking is terrible, I'm well aware, thank you."

"How are things with you and Sam?"

Jess looked over where Sam was cutting back weeds close to the house, sweat-slicked muscles singing their siren song and tempting Jess at every turn. "Good. It's nice to have a friend. Someone who knows me."

I want more.

"Good, I'm glad," Celia softly said. "How are things with Momma? Any changes? Anything I should know about?"

"Pretty much the same since you dropped me off." Jess tried and failed to keep the bitter edge out of her voice. "We're waiting on a shower chair apparently, and I'm just trying to keep the house going. Sam offered to fix up the car."

"Please just make sure you have someone to watch Momma if you need to leave. She might fall or get hurt if left alone," Celia pleaded.

"I'm not going to leave her alone." Jess rubbed the back of her neck. "I'm not wildly incompetent, you know?"

Celia sighed. "I know that. I'm just worried. This is a lot of responsibility—"

"And I'm irresponsible," Jess spat.

"I didn't say that," Celia snapped. "I'm saying I know this is a lot of stress and I'm worried it might be too much for you—"

"Funny, I would've thought we'd have this conversation before you made the unilateral decision that I would be the one to move home."

"Please, Jess, I don't want to argue every single time we talk."

Jess shrugged and dropped her arms down to her sides as if Celia could see her frustration. "Well, maybe you shouldn't treat me like an idiot."

"I don't think you're an idiot, Jess, I'm sorry," Celia said. "I just wanted to call and check on things and see if you needed anything. I'd like to come down soon with the kids. Maybe they could get to know their aunt."

Jess chewed on her bottom lip. "Yeah, I'm sure Momma would like that too."

"Great." Celia sighed in relief. "I'm going to go then. I love you, Jess."

Jess hesitated a moment, fingers tightening around the phone. "Yeah," she murmured. "Love you too."

Sam leaned the weed whacker against the porch railing and watched Jess pace a path into the freshly cut grass. She wasn't close enough that Sam could hear the entire conversation with Celia, but Jess' body language was enough of an indication. Those two always argued. Even when they got along, they argued. Most of the time about little shit. Sometimes about big shit. Sam stayed out of it most of the time, electing to let them handle it however they wanted to. A method that usually worked unless they decided to scrap.

"The more things seem to change, the more they stay the same," Juniper tsked, shaking her head.

"Think they'll be able to get through a conversation without arguing?" Sam asked, dabbing her head with a towel she kept around her neck.

"Water is wet, the sky is blue, and sisters argue. Your aunt Ramona and I have had our fair share of fights." Juniper chuckled. "Anyway, lunch is ready, go get your father off that thing so y'all can wash up."

Sam walked around to the background and flagged down her father, waiting for him to turn the mower her direction and stop a few feet away. "Momma said lunch is ready."

"Oh good." Keith hopped down from the mower with surprising ease. It always surprised everyone how nimble Keith was given his sheer size. He was strong but also knew how to move himself fast should he need to.

Jess was already inside, hands freshly washed, pouring glasses full of ice-cold iced tea, plopping a lemon wedge into every glass but one—she squeezed the lemon wedge into Aveline's and tossed the crushed wedge into her own glass. The scent of tart apples and cinnamon lingered in the air but the pie cooling on the counter wasn't for lunch. Juniper glared at Keith when his eyes lingered too long on the pie. No words needed. Keith sighed heavily and turned away from the pie while washing his hand in the sink.

Sam snorted. She loved her parents. Loved the perceived ease of their relationship. They knew each other in high school but didn't date and marry until their early twenties. They never argued. Sam never had to hide away in her room and cover her ears to quell the shouting because they never fought. Disagreements were easily squashed and at the end of the day, they showed their children how much they loved each other.

It had taken Sam a long time to realize how lucky she was to have parents who didn't secretly despise each other.

"The weeds choked out your garden, Momma," Jess said, cutting her mother's egg salad sandwich into squares before setting the plate in front of her.

"Oh, dear, not my flowers," Aveline murmured, shaky fingers plucking at her sandwich. "It took me years to get those flowers to come back every year."

"Wasn't the Reverend's son supposed to be taking care of your yard, Aveline?" Juniper asked.

"Was he?"

"I believe so."

Aveline huffed. "Can't trust that boy to do anything he's told unless it's his pecker doing the talking."

Jess and Sam choked on their sandwiches while Keith roared with laughter.

"Momma, we're at the table," Jess hissed, looking torn at whether she should laugh or not.

"It's my table, Jessamine."

Jess took a sip of her tea and shook her head. "Anyway, I was going to ask if you wanted me to try replanting anything once I clear out the weeds."

"If you can manage to keep them alive."

Jess rolled her eyes. "Can't cook, can't garden—why don't you just take me out back and shoot me?"

Juniper patted her hand. "Now, now, no need for that," she chuckled. "There are plenty of hardy plants that don't need much."

"Might want to wait until after this hurricane," Keith interjected. "They think it might hit us next weekend."

"Don't you cuss at this table, Keith Williams; the last thing we need is a hurricane," Juniper snapped.

"How are you in hurricane supplies?" Sam asked, gently nudging Jess with her elbow.

"I have to look. I didn't see any supplies in the back room, but there might be some in the attic—"

"You stay the hell out of that attic, Jessamine," Aveline said.

Jess frowned. "Why?"

"There are no hurricane supplies and it's not safe for you to go up there."

Jess tapped her fingers on the table. "Yeah, okay."

Sam knew Jess-speak well. Nothing was okay and she was going to snoop around that attic first chance she got. Not that Sam could blame her as Sam's curiosity was also piqued by Aveline's abrupt order condemning that attic—a space that Sam had never given a second thought to until now.

"What do you think is in there?" Sam asked her when they were back outside and their hands in the weeds.

"I'm going to find out."

"Obviously."

Jess huffed a laugh. "I swear Momma doesn't know me at all. She says not to do something as if she thinks I'm going to listen to her." She tossed a bunch of weeds over her shoulder, dirt sprinkling down her shirt. "Maybe there's some awful secret up there."

"Like what?"

Jess shrugged. "Maybe something about daddy."

Sam didn't know what to say. Jess' father—as far as anyone knew—had skipped out on them when Jess was seven. And before then, Juniper often woke up him late at night, ushering a crying Celia and Jess into the room with the girls. Though Jess often snuck away to crawl into bed with Sam until she stopped crying and fell asleep. Juniper always knew. Never said anything. Sam provided comfort that Jess had trouble finding elsewhere, and Sam liked providing it.

"Have you ever heard of someone named Lottie?" Jess asked, pivoting in another direction so fast that Sam needed a moment to catch up.

"Lottie? No, why?"

"Momma's called me Lottie a couple of times." Jess straightened with her hands on her hips. "It's weird. She says things like 'he won't like it if he finds out, Lottie' and things like that. I have to remind her I'm Jess, but she just...acts strange. As if she's dreaming or something."

"Or sleepwalking."

"More awake than that I think."

Sam hummed. "Might just be a side effect of the dementia. Maybe Lottie is someone she knew."

"Maybe, but just...the whole thing is weird." Jess shook her head. "Like who is she? She was looking at Pawpaw's room, but I don't ever remember Pawpaw being mean or anything. He was always nice to me and Celia."

Sam didn't remember much about the man herself. He often stayed on the porch and watched the kids when they played outside or in the pond, always keeping a close eye on his granddaughters. One night Keith had gotten a call and rushed out, and the next day Sam woke to the news that Jess' grandad had gone missing during a hunting trip. Everyone helped search for him, but their town was surrounded by woods that stretched on for miles and miles before thinning out into another town.

No one ever found him.

"I don't think asking will get me anywhere," Jess muttered, grabbing a handful of stubborn sweetgrass and digging her heels in to rip it out. Green stained her fingers.

"Probably not."

Weeds gave way to damp soil. Thin worms wriggled their starving bodies into the disturbed piles, burrowing ever deeper for more nutrients than the weeds provided. Unfortunately for them, thick red clay lingered a few feet down in the soil. Jess tossed the piles into the drainage ditch between her property and the dirt road. Half of the ditch was a verdant green while the other half was full of blackened detritus on top of dry soil—evidence of the years of burning.

"Probably have to burn after the hurricane," Jess mumbled. "Which I'm hoping they're wrong about by the way. The last thing I want to do is ride out a storm with Momma."

"I can stay," Sam blurted out before she thought about it.

"What?"

Sam cleared her throat, red staining the back of her neck but she could pretend it was from the sun. "If you're worried, I can stay with you if the hurricane hits. Just in case."

She waited for Jess to say no.

"That makes sense, and I'm sure staying in your trailer would be dangerous," Jess murmured.

"Momma would make me come stay with her."

"Do you think she'd be okay if you stayed with me instead?"

"Is that a yes?"

"Did you think it wouldn't be?"

"A bit."

Jess' fingers brushed Sam's. "I want you to stay," she whispered.

Sam looked down at how close their hands were. Jess' pinky brushed Sam's thumb and Sam wanted to entwine their fingers together. Would it feel the same? Different? Better?

"Ready to swim?" Jess asked, oblivious to Sam's inner turmoil.

Sam mutely followed Jess down the sloping backyard to the gnarled roots of the willow trees. Low-hanging branches wept thin leaves onto their shoulders as they ducked underneath. Jess stripped down first, peeling off her thin tank top and tossing it onto a large root. Her shorts followed. The plain black bikini clung to Jess' breasts and hips. Jess had always been soft, but she was even more so now, a small stretch of stomach hanging over the waistband of the bikini, and stretch marks decorating from her breasts and down to her thighs.

Sam felt as if she had stuffed a carton of cotton balls in her mouth. She tried to swallow but her throat caught.

"You okay?" Jess asked, pulling stray leaves from Sam's hair.

When had she moved so close? Did she know how badly Sam wanted to touch her? Peel the bathing suit away from Jess' sweat-slick skin and refresh her memory on how Jess' felt pressed against her. Soft sunlight through the willows, ensconcing Jess in a gentle glow. A sign from God if Sam ever saw one.

Jess was made for worship and Sam was ready to pray.

Chapter 6

JESS WAITED UNTIL AVELINE dozed off in her recliner. Belly full of decaf coffee and maple and brown sugar oatmeal luring her to sleep. When she was sure Momma was asleep, Jess crept up the stairs to look in the one place Aveline had barred her from entering.

The attic.

She had held off snooping around for a few days, just in case Momma remembered her warning and kept a close eye on Jess. But she seemed to have forgotten as quickly as she spat out the command. Dementia—a blessing in this particular instance. On the third day, Jess acted normally. She woke Momma and got her ready for the day, fed her breakfast, and got her settled. Even did some light cleaning in the living room—dusting the small porcelain knick-knacks scattered on the TV and buffet—while waiting for Aveline's eyelids to flutter closed.

The pull cord swung listlessly in the hallway, a temptation for days, and Jess stood on the balls of her feet to snatch it. She carefully opened the hatch and lowered the ladder. Her foot pressed the bottom rung, testing the wood and hoping it would hold her. Each rung felt damp and pliable, more than likely rotten from a build of moisture in the attic. Jess scurried up the ladder before any of them broke.

Cardboard boxes crumbled, leaving moth-eaten blankets spilling out across the old boards. A fake Christmas tree was abandoned in the corner covered in cobwebs and a thick layer of dust. The totes with white tape labels fared better than the boxes. Jess carefully walked past the ones labeled HOLIDAY DECORATIONS and DADDY'S THINGS—unsure if that meant Jess' father or Pawpaw—and found the one unmarked faded green tote. Her heart quivered in excitement and trepidation.

She could unearth a major secret. Something that could destroy their already fractured family. That didn't stop Jess. She carefully fit her fingers under the lid and...

Huffed in disappointment.

Nothing more than an unlabeled box of Celia's old porcelain dolls that she had grown out of when they were teenagers, still packaged in their boxes.

She turned to go back downstairs when a small chest caught her eye. The scroll work on the front reminded her of the flowers Pawpaw had carved into Momma's dresser. She brushed her fingers over the rusted lock. The chest wasn't large. Small enough for her to tuck it under arm and carry it down the ladder. She left it in her room until she could figure out a way to open it and quietly closed the attic.

All was quiet as Jess tiptoed down the stairs and turned into the living room to check on Momma, but Aveline wasn't in her chair.

"Fuck!"

Jess whirled around to check the doors and make sure Momma hadn't wandered out the door and jumped back until she slammed into the door frame.

Aveline narrowed her eyes. "Watch your language, missy," she mumbled, standing in the hall with a record in her hands.

"I thought you had walked off," Jess argued but there was no bite in it. She pressed her hand to her pounding heart.

"I am capable of walking," Aveline sniped.

Jess rolled her eyes, worry seeping away quickly. "I know that, Momma, that's the scary part."

Aveline pushed past, pursing her lips, and stopped in the middle of the living room. "Jessamine, where is the record player? I wanted to play some music."

"You threw it out years ago, remember?" Jess leaned against the frame with her arms crossed. "It stopped working and you threw it into the ditch while calling it a miserable piece of shit."

"Well, that doesn't sound like me."

"It was daddy's."

"Oh." Aveline on the edge of her recliner, record in her lap. "I suppose that does sound right then."

"Why did daddy leave?" Jess asked, doubting Momma would tell her. Both she and Celia had asked for years but Aveline never cracked, and they never got their answer.

"He was a miserable lout."

Jess sighed. "I don't know why I asked."

"Because you're hoping I'll have an answer that's going to make you feel better and there isn't one."

"Then what's the truth," Jess challenged.

"That is the truth." Aveline leaned back in the recliner. "Your father didn't understand that having children means they come first ahead of your wants, and he decided he didn't want to try and play house anymore. I didn't stop him."

Momma was right. That didn't make Jess feel better. She couldn't understand having children and not loving them wholly. Why go through the pain of carrying and labor and bringing new life into the world, and then not give a fuck? Jess' fingers strayed to her stomach before she shook them and shoved her hand into her pocket.

"I'll be right back," she said.

The old boombox she and Celia had saved up for by mowing lawns and working the ice cream shop in the summer sat on the dresser, covered in peeling stickers. Jess carried it downstairs and plugged it in the living room.

"None of that rock and roll stuff you kids listen to," Aveline said.

"Rock and roll started in your era, Momma," Jess teasingly reminded her, switching through stations until Patsy Cline crooned through the speaker. "Here."

Aveline sighed with a soft smile. "Thank you, Jessamine."

"You're welcome."

Aveline hummed along and Jess left her alone in the living room. While she could ask about the chest it might squander the non-argumentative moment they just shared. Jess didn't want to ruin the kernel of peace.

The phone rang and Jess grabbed the cordless, hoping to hear Sam's voice on the other end.

"Jess, honey, I'm so glad you answered," Nancy's high-pitched voice made Jess wince. "I just saw the weather report and wanted to call you."

"Oh—"

"Did you see it, dear? A category three coming right for us by Sunday! Supposed to be terrible winds and rain, and as soon as I saw it, I just knew I had to call you," she kept going, not letting Jess get a word in edgewise. "Of course you and your Momma can come stay with me—"

Absolutely not.

"We've got enough supplies and y'all can share the guest bed. I would be so worried if y'all were in the house all by yourselves. Lord, what if something happened?"

Nancy finally stopped to draw breath and Jess jumped in before Nancy could prattle on again: "Actually, Sam will be staying with us during the storm just in case, and we have supplies."

A lie, but Jess would have supplies by the time the storm hit.

Nancy was stunned into silence and Jess tried to keep her laugh inside. They had really thought Jess wouldn't accept Sam back so easily, but they didn't know her at all. Sam could tell her to jump, and Jess would ask how high.

"Oh, well, isn't that nice?" Nancy finally forced out, words stilted. "Are you and Sam...?"

As much as Jess wanted to brag that they were back together as if nothing had changed, she didn't want to do something like that without Sam's permission.

"We're friends. I'm so happy we've had the chance to reconnect again," Jess said instead. "Sam is amazing, and I've missed having her in my life."

"W-well, i-if you need anything, dear—"

"I'll be sure to call," Jess let her voice get slow and sweet like molasses in January. "Have a good day."

Jess ended the call with a satisfied click. A feeling that didn't last long as the hurricane landed on her already full plate. There definitely hadn't been any supplies in the attic and she had searched in the closets and the backroom. She found a flashlight with no batteries and a few candles. They needed far more than that to weather a storm.

Loretta Lynn sang while Jess opened the pantry to take stock of non-perishables. She snagged a can of peaches. The smeared black ink of the good by date had passed several years ago. Jess winced. Several other cans of fruits and vegetables were the same. She dragged over the trash can and began tossing out of date cans, which ended being almost all of them.

Checking the cans turned into check the boxed goods, all out of date as well, emptying the shelves quickly. Jess popped open the tin of flour. Tiny black specks crawled amongst the white and she groaned.

Fucking weevils.

She overturned the tin into the trash, dust puffing into the air like a cloud, and she tossed the tin in the sink. Everyone could bring by food but none of them thought to check the bug-infested food in the pantry.

By the time Jess was finished, they had two cans of cooked ham and a tin of sardines that she also tossed in the trash because she was not eating those. She tied up the trash and tossed it into the bin outside, making a mental note to ask Sam to help her haul the trash down to the dump before the storm. Picking up scattered trash after a storm was her least favorite activity.

Cleaning out the pantry turned into Jess wiping down the shelves with soapy water. Dried out bug husks, their legs curled tight to their still bodies, and dirt swam in the water until she changed out the water and wiped the shelves a second time.

Down on her hands and knees, she saw it.

Dark brown spots dotted the baseboards like freckles. She brushed her fingers over them, expecting them to come away like flecks of dirt. Several passes with the soapy rag succeeded in scrubbing away bits of paint but the spots remained. Jess leaned back on her ankles and frowned. She desperately hoped it wasn't mold. A difficult problem she didn't have the fortitude or money to solve.

Bleach made her head swim as she donned gloves and scrubbed at the spots, praying to a God that never listened to her anyway, that they would disappear. She cussed under her breath.

"I don't think cussing at them is going to make them go away."

Jess jumped, knocking her head on the bottom shelf. "Fuck!" Stars burst in her eyes.

Sam's calloused hands cradled Jess' cheeks before sinking into her hair and feeling for the tender spot on Jess' scalp. "Sorry." She kissed the top of Jess' head. "I didn't mean to scare you."

Heat worked its way up Jess' neck, staining her cheeks a faint pink. "It's okay. I didn't hear you come in."

"Too busy cussing at..." Sam trailed off and leaned down to look. "Shit, I hope that isn't mold."

"My thought exactly."

Sam brushed her fingers over the spots. "Seems more like water damage possibly."

"Is that easier to fix?"

"It can be." Sam hesitated. "Or it could be a larger problem. I won't know unless I cut into it. Might have to crawl under the house since it seems like it's coming up rather than in."

Jess huffed. "I can't ask you do that."

"Who says you need to ask?" Sam grinned and ruffled Jess' hair. "We'll figure it out. Now come on out before you make yourself pass out."

Jess took Sam's offered hand and took a deep breath once she stood in the kitchen. "I forget how potent bleach is."

Sam pulled out a chair and Jess plopped down, stretching out her aching knees, and Sam sat next to her. "You've kept busy today," Sam said, nudging Jess' ankle with her boot.

"Starting look for anything we can use for supplies and ended up tossing everything."

"Guess we'll have to go shopping then."

Jess turned her head and looked at the small clock hanging above the phone. "Derotha will be here in a bit. I'm sure she wouldn't mind us making a quick trip while she tends to Momma."

"Are you sure you want me to go with you?"

"Why wouldn't I?"

Sam shrugged in an effort to look nonchalant, but her eyes drifted away from Jess. "They'll never stop talking about you. Never let you forget you were walking about with a tranny. The whispers in church will be louder than the good Reverend's sermon."

Jess snorted. "Unlikely."

But Sam didn't laugh.

Jess leaned forward, reaching for Sam's hand—the one that brushed through Jess' hair and cradled her face with softness Jess didn't think she deserved. "When have I ever given a damn what any of these people think of me?"

Sam stared down at their joined hands. "It's different this time, they'll think..."

"They'll think what?"

"That we're together again. That you're fucking a tranny—"

"Stop saying it like that."

"I'm saying it how they're going to say it to you when they accuse you of loving me," Sam snapped. "They'll loudly whisper it behind your back wherever you go. Maybe someone will actually have the gall to ask you what it's like. They'll accuse you of loving a freak of nature. A mistake."

"Are you afraid I'll say I don't love you?"

Sam didn't answer.

The distance between them disappeared by inches. So close their lips almost brushed. Jess wanted them to. Desperately. She craved Sam in a way she hadn't thought she'd be able to anymore. Didn't think she would trust anyone enough ever again. But Sam was safety. Was home. Even after their time apart, Jess couldn't help but fall back into old feelings. A fly caught in the swirl of water down the drain, helplessly buzzing and unable to fly free. She was ready to fall into Sam.

A knock came from the front door and the moment was broken. Lost. Jess sighed and stood up to wave Derotha in from the porch.

"Hey darlin'—oh hey, Sam." Derotha's voice didn't lose her cheerful edge. She didn't seem surprised nor disgusted to find Sam sitting at the kitchen table. "Been awhile since I've seen you, honey, how's your momma?"

"She's doing good, Miss Derotha." Sam answered, softly tilting her head to hide the disappointment in her eyes.

"Good, good. I'll have to give her a call when I'm not so darn busy."

Jess rubbed her grimy fingers over her shirt. "Sam offered to take me into town to get supplies. Would you mind watching—"

Derotha was waving her hands at Jess before she could even finish. "Go, go. Lord knows, you need an opportunity to get out of this house."

"I'll go clean up then."

Jess showered quickly, rinsing the smell of bleach from her hair and replacing it with the cheap strawberry shampoo she loved. She pulled on plain black shorts—the waistband rolled up in the hopes Sam wanted to look at her thighs—and a red ribbed tank top. Flip flops smacked against the wood as she met Sam at the bottom of the stairs. She grabbed Momma's pocketbook from where it hung by the door and made sure the checkbook was inside. Derotha waved them out the door with a knowing smile.

"Hold on," Sam muttered before Jess reached for the handle to the truck and hopped into the driver's side first to open the passenger door from the inside.

"Didn't you fix that?" Jess hopped up into the seat and buckled herself in.

"Several times." Sam fiddled with the radio dial before switching to the Nirvana cassette already in the player. "I've replaced that handle more times than I can count. It'll work for a bit and then break again. I sort of gave up."

Jess hummed under her breath. The truck hadn't changed much. The radio looked fairly recent but everything else looked the same. The same notches she had carved in the dashboard—right above the glove box—as a joke were all still there. She traced her fingers over the grooves and counted them. Six. One for each time she and Sam had done something in the truck that would make the good Lord turn his gaze and blush. Jess turned to say something, and Sam quickly turned her head away to look at the road, pink tinging the curve of her ear.

"I missed this truck," Jess said instead of teasing her, pleased that Sam remembered as well as she did. "I remember all the times we used to skip. Sometimes we'd just drive and listen to music."

Sam cracked a soft smile. "All that skipping, you'd think we'd fail."

"You?" Jess playfully scoffed. "You could never step foot in that school and still manage to pass nearly everything."

"You didn't do too bad yourself if memory serves."

"I did well in everything except math and chemistry." Jess shuddered. "I don't know what it is about numbers that trips me up."

"Can't be good at everything."

"I'm not good at much."

Sam pulled into the sparsely filled parking lot of the grocery store. "That's not true, Jess. You just don't give yourself enough credit for the things you are good at."

Sam was out of the truck and waiting on the sidewalk before Jess could even attempt to argue. And she was going to.

"Running away is cheating," Jess said, side-eyeing Sam as the automatic doors whooshed open and air conditioning ruffled her damp hair.

Sam chuckled. "Is it?"

Jess lightly smacked Sam's shoulder while they grabbed a cart. Only two lanes were open. Both cashiers—teenagers Jess couldn't place at first glance—stared at Sam with open expressions of disgust that churned in Jess' stomach. She wanted to snap at them. Tell them to take a picture; it would last longer since they wanted to be rude assholes.

If the looks bothered Sam, she didn't show it. She led Jess through the stocked produce section—hardly anyone bought fresh produce when a storm was coming through—and grabbed a mixed bag of apples and oranges.

"Making sure I'm getting my vitamin C," Jess teased, trying to ignore the eyes on her back.

"Something like that."

"Does it bother you?"

"The stares?"

Jess nodded.

"Yes and no." Sam pushed the cart down the water aisle. "I'm getting used to them, but some days they hurt more than others."

"I'm sorry."

Sam shrugged and grabbed a case of water jugs while Jess grabbed the packs of bottled water.

"The price of being different," Sam said.

"Small-minded jerks."

"Is the city any different?"

Jess turned the corner to the canned goods aisle. "Sort of. There are more people so there's more chances of finding people that are accepting. More opportunities to date people that are like you. I found a couple people."

Sam paused for a moment, expression unreadable. "Did you?"

Jess nodded, crouching down to reach for cans of ravioli in red sauce. "I dated a few different people. Especially when I worked at the bar. Night life was always busy. Always bringing someone new to me."

"What was her name?" Sam whispered so no one else would hear.

Jess held up a can of spaghetti rings with meatballs—she didn't like them, but Sam used to—and Sam nodded. "Her name was Sara. We saw each other for a few months before she had to move for a job."

"You didn't go with her?"

"Wasn't that kind of relationship."

"Ah."

Jess curled her fingers around the cold metal of the cart. "Have you ever...?"

"Had a relationship like that?"

She nodded.

"A few." Sam held up a can of Spam and waited for Jess to nod. "There's a community over in Wilmington. Ben and Misty went with me a few times when I was too nervous to go myself. I met some people. Learned a lot about myself."

"I'm happy you had that."

"Me too." Sam followed Jess down to the snack aisle. "There was a time when I considered moving there."

"Why didn't you?"

"Mom and pop accepted me. If they hadn't, I would've packed up and gone, but when they told me they loved me no matter what, I decided to stay." Sam's fingers brushed a damp tendril of hair behind Jess' ear. "I'm glad I did if it meant seeing you again."

Jess reached for Sam's hand and intertwined their fingers. She didn't give a shit if anyone saw. And if they were stupid enough to say something, she'd have no problem cleaning their clocks.

"I'm glad you stayed too. I don't know what I'd do if you weren't still here," Jess admitted.

Sam squeezed her hand, but her smile faltered.

Reverend Daniels stood at the end of the aisle, right next to the packages of cookies, a look of stern disappointment plain on his face. Sam tried to wriggle her hands out of Jess' grip, but Jess didn't let go. The Reverend's eyes moved down to their joined hands and his lips grew even thinner.

"Jess," he said evenly.

"Reverend."

"How's your Momma?" he asked, his eyes flicked to Sam while Sam stared at the assortment of chips to her left.

Jess plastered a fake smile on her face. "She's just fine. Miss Derotha is watching her while Sam and I shop for hurricane supplies. We were all out of everything."

"Well, that's very nice of him," the Reverend said but his face betrayed that he didn't think it was very nice at all.

Sam stiffened and Jess clenched her teeth so hard she was afraid they might crack. "*She* is wonderful. A true friend to me. Now, if you don't mind, we have to finish up here and grab dinner so Miss Derotha can get home."

Red peeked over the Reverend's starch-pressed white collar and he nodded. "Of course. And if you need anything Jess—"

"I'll be sure to call," she lied.

"Fucking asshole," Jess spat when the Reverend disappeared down a different aisle.

Sam didn't say anything. The cart squeaked as she pushed it down the aisle, waiting for Jess to fill it with whatever she needed and wanted for riding out the storm. Jess didn't know what to say. What would make Sam feel better. Every platitude died on her tongue.

"Don't forget those wine cooler things you like," Sam murmured.

"Not sure Momma would consider those necessary."

"No, but it couldn't hurt to have a little buzz now and again."

Jess couldn't argue with that logic. She grabbed a pack each of peach and strawberry. It would be nice to have them. To be able to offer Sam a drink. Maybe convince her to stay.

The cashier's upper lip curled as if she were going to say something but Jess fixed her with a glare that dared the bitch to open her mouth. Jess slid a check across the counter while Sam bagged up the groceries and wheeled the cart out the door to the truck. While the cashier had the good sense to keep her mouth shut, Jess still flipped her the bird on the way out the door.

"Want to pop over to the diner and pick up dinner?" Jess asked. "My treat."

Sam locked the groceries in the back of the truck. "Sure, but you don't have to pay for it."

"I want to."

They left the truck and walked the block to the diner, hands brushing but neither reaching for the other. Jess wasn't afraid to hold Sam's hand in view of everyone, but Sam was hesitant. She held open the door for Jess, eyes darting around to take in who might be judging them while they waited, and followed Jess to the counter. Jess slid onto the peeling red stool and leaned on the counter with her elbows. Sam remained standing.

In the corner booth, sat a few of the ladies from the church auxiliary. A fancy name to indicate they were the busy bodies of the holy building. Nancy sat in the middle of them, her pink lips pursed in a similar manner as the Reverend's had been. They both oozed the same mixture of disappointment and disgust.

"What can I get you, darlin'?" Darlene asked, pulling the pink pen from behind her ear. Silver hair was coiffed in a near perfect beehive. Jess had never seen her in a different hair style. She often wondered if Darlene's hair had stiffened into that permanent shape from the years of hairspray.

"Taking some dinner home for us and Momma," Jess said. "Do you have any hummingbird cake made?"

"Cake isn't dinner, Jess," Darlene gently chastised, her red lips curved in a smile. "But yes, we do. Some for you too, Sam?"

Sam nodded. "Yes, ma'am."

"Alright, now what do you want that's actually a meal?"

Jess ordered Momma's favorite—country fried steak with mashed potatoes and green beans with bacon—wanting to give the woman something to eat that wasn't a casserole or day-old fried chicken while Jess and Sam picked food they wanted to split as they always did. They settled on a double bacon cheeseburger with mac and cheese and fried okra, and a spicy fried chicken sandwich with seasoned fries and fried pickles. Jess kicked her legs while they waited, her fingers itching to grab Sam's.

Hushed whispers from the corner booth slowly spoiled her good mood.

"Do you see what that girl is wearing?"

"If Aveline weren't senile she'd never let that girl walk out of the house like that."

"Such a shame."

"Still a troublemaker after all these years."

Each whisper stuck in Jess' jaw, making it tighten. She gnashed her teeth together. Her fingers drummed against the counter, moving faster and faster the more agitated she got.

"Girls like that deserve exactly what's coming to them," a low voice hissed in her ear.

Jess whirled around. "What the fuck did you just say?"

The ladies froze. Nancy's mouth was set in a perfect "o" of surprise, her hand resting on her breastbone to clutch the invisible pearls over Jess being crass enough to cuss in public.

"W-we didn't say anything, hun," Nancy stammered, blinking her eyes in feigned innocence. "Are you alright, Jess? You look a bit peaked."

Jess moved to slide off the stool—her hands curled into fists and ready to swing—but Sam stopped her with an arm around her waist. How dare they act as if they didn't say something awful about her? They couldn't even have the courage to say it to her face.

"Don't let them get to you," Sam whispered in Jess' ear. "Not a damn one of them is worth you losing your temper, baby."

Jess wasn't so sure. These women said whatever they wanted because they hadn't been popped in the mouth nearly enough. Jess was willing to perform that service. Maybe they'd learn to stop talking about people behind their backs.

"Please don't haul off and hit that woman," Darlene pleaded, setting two plastic bags on the counter. "Trust me, I know the temptation, but I'd hate to ban you from the diner."

Jess sighed. "Fine."

"Good girl." Darlene reached over and patted her hand. "Now, I packed up some extra gravy for your Momma, and extra pickles for you and Sam."

"Thanks, Darlene."

"You two take good care of each other, now," Darlene winked.

Sam guided Jess out of the store, keeping a hand on her elbow as they walked past the judgmental stares from the corner booth, waiting until they were outside to grasp Jess' hand in hers.

"Thanks," Jess said. "God, that woman pisses me off."

"I know." Sam squeezed her hand.

"Her saying that to me just set me off. That girls like me deserve what's coming to us." She blew out a breath. "It's such a shitty thing to say."

Sam frowned. "I didn't hear her say that."

"What?"

"I heard the other things about your outfit and your momma not letting you out of the house but I didn't hear that one. Maybe, I—"

Sam jolted to a stop a few feet away from the truck, her eyes growing glassy. One the side of the truck, in red paint so fresh that it looked like dripping blood, were the words DIE TRANNY.

Sam dragged her fingers over the rusty lock. She rubbed the orange-red flecks from her fingers and leaned back in the kitchen chair. "No key?"

Jess swallowed a mouthful of the sicky sweet peach wine cooler and shook her head. "None that I could see."

Sam hummed. As soon as they had made it back to the house, Sam had asked to borrow the hose and spray off what she could of the paint smeared on her truck. The words bled together and stained the green grass. Jess didn't give a damn. She wanted them gone though they had already done damage. Sam barely spoke while they ate. She stayed and helped put things away and then waited quietly while Jess tucked her mother into bed and dashed upstairs for the chest. Jess wished she knew how to take this hurt away.

"I could break it open. Would be easy enough," Sam murmured. "Do you have an idea what's in here?"

Jess shook her head.

With a screwdriver and a hammer, Sam popped the hinges off and carefully pulled the top open. Their shoulders touched as they looked into the chest. A small white photo album sat on top of a checkered piece of fabric. Jess pulled out the album first while Sam reached for the fabric. The soft pink cotton unfurled to reveal a dress with a white bow around the waist. If Jess had to guess by size, it couldn't be for anyone older than a child or young teen. Sam sucked in a breath.

"What?" Jess asked.

Sam turned the dress around to show the back and Jess leaned away on instinct. A brown stain spread through the fabric of the skirt. She hoped it was mud.

"Who keeps a dress like this?" Sam asked, carefully placing it back in the chest.

"Momma's never mentioned it before." Jess flipped open the album to black and white pictures with yellowed edges.

"Recognize anyone?"

Jess tapped a picture of a young man, eyes bright as he smiled, with his arm around a woman she didn't recognize. "I think this is Pawpaw, and maybe my grandmother?"

"She died before you were born, didn't she?"

Jess nodded and flipped the page. A child of roughly ten grinned up at the camera with her arm around a girl who looked similar. Same dark eyes and upturned nose as Jess. "I think this is Momma when she was younger."

Sam rested her chin on Jess' shoulder and Jess' heart rattled in its cage. "Who's that girl with her?"

"I don't know." Jess found more pictures of them together. She stopped at a picture of them both wearing checkered dresses with bows around the waist and matching buckled shoes. She pulled the picture from the sleeve and flipped it around. "Aveline and Charlotte."

"Charlotte?"

Jess placed the picture back in the sleeve. "Do you think Charlotte is Lottie?"

Sam sat up and Jess swallowed her protest. "It's plausible. Not sure if asking her is a good idea."

"No?"

"I think this might be a memory chest, Jess. For when someone dies."

Jess swallowed. "Oh. No, then it probably wouldn't be a good idea." She closed the album and carefully placed it back on top of the dress. "Lottie must've been a good friend of hers for her to have this."

"Probably."

Silence stretched between them. Jess wished she knew what to say. Everything that came to mind felt inadequate.

Sam looked at the clock over the phone. "It's getting late. I should probably go."

Don't go. Stay.

"Yeah, you're right. I'm sure you have things to do," Jess murmured. "Thank you for everything today."

Sam stood and stretched, gathering her tools. "No problem. I'll check in tomorrow, but I promised Pop I'd help him at the house."

Jess nodded mutely.

"Goodnight, Jess."

"Night, Sam."

The screen door swung shut with a soft thump and Jess sighed, chugging down the dregs of the fizzy peach drink. She rinsed the bottle in the sink. No ants were gonna make a home in her trash until she could get it to the dump. The screen door creaked again, and Jess heard Sam step back into the kitchen.

She set the bottle on the counter and turned. "Forget some—"

Sam's hands cradled her face. Thumbs dug into her cheeks. Lips met hers. Soft. Scared. Trembling against her mouth. Electricity sparked in her brain. Synapses fired in overdrive. Butterflies erupted and flooded her belly. Jess reached. Fingers tangling in Sam's hair. She balanced on the balls of her feet. Sam tasted of toasted pecans and sweet cream cheese frosting, mingling with the syrup that still coated Jess' tongue.

The counter dug into Jess' back. Time lost all meaning. They could have been there for hours. Jess wouldn't have minded. She had half a mind to beg Sam to stay. For the night. Forever.

Sam pulled away first, forehead resting against Jess'. "I've been wanting to do that since I saw you that night, wearing those ridiculous gloves and my old shirt."

"You could've," Jess murmured, tilting her head back, eyes begging for another kiss. "I wouldn't have minded."

Sam laughed. "If that's the case, I hope you don't if I kiss you again."

"You can kiss me all you like."

"I'll be sure to take you up on that."

Chapter 7

WIND WHIPPED THE BRANCHES of the trees into a frenzy. Leaves ripped through the air and scattered over the yard and the frothy surface of the pond. Tiny slivers plastered themselves to the windows. Jess poured three cups of coffee as Sam's truck rumbled down the road and pulled into the spot beside Momma's car. Power had flickered a few times as strong gusts buffeted the house, but still held on for dear life.

Fingers brushed over her neck, pushing her hair away to make space for a small kiss beneath her earlobe.

"Sorry, I'm late," Sam murmured against Jess' skin. "Lily decided to sneak off to her boyfriend's and I had to go tell her to take her ass home before Momma had an aneurysm."

Jess giggled. "She's pulling the same shit you did at her age."

"Yeah, and Jack was always running after me to pull me back home by the back of my damn neck." Sam dropped a kiss to Jess' shoulder, arms snaking around Jess' waist. "You look beautiful today."

"I look the same as I do every day," Jess scoffed and tugged at the edge of her faded t-shirt.

"Exactly."

Jess laughed and clicked off the coffee pot, pushing it back into its normal spot on the counter. "I made your coffee. Figure we might as well get one cup in at least before the power goes out."

"Maybe it won't this time."

The power gave out shortly after dinner, which was longer than Jess expected it to last, during an episode of Wheel of Fortune when Jess was on the cusp of solving the puzzle. They had spent most of the day watching TV for lack of something better to do. Jess had dozed off more than once, her head in Sam's lap and Sam's fingers brushing through her hair.

Wind howled around the house. Beams trembled and the house shook. Jess half-expected the wind to curl under the edges of the roof and rip it right off. Most it had ever done—thankfully—was rip off some shingles and fling them around the yard. Rain pattered against the window, lighter now than it had been hours ago.

"I'll get the candles," Jess mumbled, standing up from the couch and stretching her arms over her head until her back popped.

"Do you need help?" Sam asked.

"No," —Jess called over the howl of wind as she opened the hall closet— "I moved them close because I knew we would probably need them."

Soft points of yellow light flickered in the slight breeze sneaking in around the windows. Jess placed just enough to illuminate the living room. Shadows danced on the edges, creeping up from the baseboards towards the ceiling. Other than the sounds of the storm outside, the house was deathly quiet. She could barely even hear her mother's soft breaths.

"I brought a weather radio," Sam said. "Left it in the truck though."

Jess snorted. "That's a great place for it."

"Ha." Sam rolled her eyes, the whites glowing yellow in the light. "I'll be right back."

"Are you sure, Sam? It's awfully windy out." Aveline plucked the loose threads on the arm of her recliner. "Don't want you to get hurt."

"Won't take more than a few seconds, Miss Aveline." Sam grabbed a flashlight by the front door.

Jess watched from the screen door, a fine mist of rain spraying her face and neck, as Sam jogged down the steps and out to her truck. The blue light of the flashlight danced across the ground and disappeared for a few seconds. Wind blocked out the sound of the truck door opening and closing. The bobbing light came back towards the house and Jess opened the door. Despite only taking a few seconds, Sam's hair was plastered to her face and neck. She closed the door.

"It's not too terrible out there, honestly," Sam said, tugging at the damp fabric of her shirt.

Jess swallowed a laugh and took the white plastic radio. "You can change into your night clothes in the bathroom. I'll set this up."

Static buzzed as she spun the dial, searching for a station. She'd hear a voice, pause, but it would be too faint to hear anything. Jess kept searching until she found the local weather broadcast, giving updates on the storm until it blew through the area and broke up into a rough gust of wind.

"Cantore is in Wilmington, sounds like," Jess said, setting the radio down on the coffee table. "Guess we know where the storm is gonna be the worst."

Aveline hummed. "I don't know whether or not that man is a fool."

"Passionate, I think."

"Until a storm sweeps him into the ocean."

Jess snorted. "You're very negative sometimes, Momma."

"Realistic, more like."

"I don't know. He's doing what he loves." Jess tucked her feet up on the couch. "Was being a mother what you wanted?"

"Of course it was."

"Really? You didn't want to be anything else?"

Aveline was silent a moment. "There were dreams. Everyone has dreams. I just learned at a young age that dreams don't pay bills or feed hungry mouths."

"Do you regret it? Not following your dream?"

"What are you really asking, Jessamine?" Aveline's eyes were sharp in the low light.

Jess shrugged. "I'm just wondering if you regret having us. I can't imagine raising us—*me*—was easy when you did it alone."

"I regret a great many things, Jessamine. Raising you, no matter how difficult you were and by God, you were, is not one of those things," Aveline murmured. "My life is what it is, and I have long since accepted that."

"Does it scare you? Forgetting?"

Aveline sighed brokenly. "All the damn time."

Jess tapped her fingers on the arm before reaching over and covering her mother's hand with hers. A hand that used to pop her on the mouth when she got fresh, scour cast irons pots and pans under blistering hot water, and pull weeds in fat bunches. Such a frail hand now. Skin paper, thin and taut over blue veins and bony knuckles.

A door softly closed down the hallway and Jess pulled her hand away as Sam walked back into the living room, wearing a pair of soft pink shorts and black tank top, and patting her damp hair dry. She perched on the edge of the couch and shot Jess a soft smile.

"Did I miss anything?" Sam asked, tilting her head towards the radio.

Jess shook her head. "Nothing important yet. It's moving ashore which we kind of already knew."

Sam snorted.

"I think I'd like to turn in early. I'm very tired," Aveline said. "You're not sleeping upstairs are you, Jessamine?"

"Of course not, Momma. Sam and I are gonna share the pullout."

"Good, good." Aveline nodded and pushed herself up, arms shaking as she braced herself on the arms of the recliner. "Help me to bed, would you?"

Jess guided Aveline down the shadowy hallway, Aveline's hand tucked in the crook of Jess' elbow, a candle held aloft in her other hand. Flame danced as Jess helped Momma change into a thin nightgown that wouldn't make her overheat while she slept without the cool night breeze. When the storm was on its way out, Jess would crack open the windows and let in the dying winds to cool the house again.

The queen-sized bed nearly swallowed Aveline. Jess pulled the thin sheet up to Aveline's chest and smoothed down the edges. Never in a million years did she think she would ever see her mother like this. So small. Diminished. The fire in Aveline's eyes barely smoldered on a good day. All of those arguments and fights over the years seemed so far away. Some completely pointless.

Aveline caught Jess' hand. "We don't always see eye to eye, no mothers and daughters do, but even on your worst day, I love you, Jessamine."

Words caught in Jess' throat. She swallowed. "I love you too, Momma."

She left the door cracked open, the baby monitor already in the living room in case Momma needed her during the night, and padded back down the hall. Sam already had the coffee table moved by the TV and was pulling the cushions off of the couch.

"Thought you might like to go ahead and get comfy," Sam said, setting the cushions aside. "And we could play a card game or something."

Jess didn't know what the "or something" option was but she was already game.

"Sure." She tried to keep the excitement out of her voice while she grabbed the metal bar and helped Sam unfold the mattress. "I can change into my PJs and be right back."

"Where are the pillows and sheets?"

"In the closet," Jess whispered over her shoulder.

The candle flickered wildly as she walked down the hallway. Shadows raced across the pictures hung on the walls and dark splotches moved down the crooked cross tacked in the middle of the wall, almost dripping from the bottom like blood or ichor. Jess straightened the cross, the wood cold to the touch despite the sticky warmth gathering in the house.

Sam had left the door to the bathroom wide open, and Jess left it that way as she stripped out of her sweaty clothes. Cold water from the tap wet a washcloth enough for Jess to wipe herself down. Her cotton nightdress hung on a hook over the bathroom door. The dress was actually one of Aveline's old ones that Jess had pilfered before she left home, and she had kept it ever since.

Red roses had long since faded to pink, the green stems barely visible anymore. Jess pulled down the hem until it skirted the tops of her knees. A small slit on either side ended mid-thigh. She straightened the inch-thick straps, running her fingers over laced edges.

Drip, drip, drip.

A chill slid down her back. She whirled, eyes darting around for the source of the sound. Her fingers reached for the candle and she held it out towards the bathtub.

Droplets of water dripped from the spigot and sent shock waves through the tub full of water. Jess heaved a sigh of relief. She leaned over to tighten the knob. The candle hovered over the water. Jess looked down.

A grotesque faced stared back at her. Flesh clinging onto bone and floating in the dark water. Wide eyes, the whites yellowed and pulsing with tiny red capillaries, unblinking up at her. Lips peeled away to reveal a row of perfectly straight teeth.

Jess clapped her hand over her mouth so she wouldn't scream, and stumbled back into the sink.

No, no, no. Not again. This can't be happening again.

She squeezed her eyes shut. Counted back from ten in her head. When she opened her eyes, it would be gone. It wasn't real. Wasn't there. She had just been freaked out by the dark. That's all. Stress had been building since she came home; it was only natural for it to hit her in unexpected ways.

Her hand shook as she held the candle over the tub. Nothing stared back up at her.

It was nothing. I'm fine. I'm fine.

Jess dragged in a deep breath and left the bathroom. See, she could handle her anxiety just fine. She didn't need doctors or pills that made her foggy and tired. Nobody had to know.

But she didn't feel better until she was back in the living room, Sam sat cross-legged on the pullout and waiting for Jess to return.

"Not the granny gown," Sam teased as Jess set down the candle and climbed onto the old, creaky mattress.

"Don't knock the granny gown," Jess shot back, avoiding the pack of Oreos and open bag of Cheetos set in the middle. "It's very comfortable."

Sam raised an eyebrow. "I'm sure it is."

"Look me in the eye and tell me it doesn't do something for you," Jess joked.

Sam snickered.

"I'm really glad you're here. Would've sucked to be here alone with no power," Jess murmured.

Sam patted Jess' knee before leaning back and reaching for the two open strawberry wine coolers on the small table by the couch. "Thought you might like a small buzz."

Strawberry syrup fizzed on her tongue and warmed its way down to her belly. "Thanks."

Sam picked up a pack of cards. "Go fish?"

"Oh, I see we're going very high stakes this evening."

"Only the best for you."

The sound of shuffling cards muffled the droning of the weatherman, repeating the same information about the storm before cutting to someone "on the scene" who no one could hear over the high winds and rain no matter how they shouted into the microphone.

"Do you miss living in the city?" Sam asked, dealing out the cards.

Jess shrugged. "Yeah. I mean, there's more to do, obviously. But it's never quiet which is fine sometimes and other times I miss the quiet."

"Did you leave a lot of friends behind?"

"Not really." Jess organized her deck from highest to low and discarded a pair of fours. "I knew a lot of people but I don't think I'd call any of them a friend. They were mostly people I drank and did stupid shit with. It's kind of sad honestly. Seven years and not one meaningful connection."

"Not even dating?"

"Most were flings. My last relationship was...I thought it was going to be more, but I was wrong. Do you have a seven?"

"Go fish." Sam brushed a wisp of hair away from her face. "Did it end badly?"

Jess nodded, not trusting herself to speak. She didn't want to talk about it. Didn't want to travel down that dark corridor in her mind. Not now. Not with Sam. Not with anyone.

"I'm sorry. Do you have a King?"

Jess handed over a card. "What about you?"

"Most of mine were flings too, I suppose. Do you have a three?"

"Go fish."

Sam pulled a card and discarded a pair. "Though, they were all meaningful to me in some way. It was so different meeting a community of people like me and exploring who I was in a more accepting environment."

"When did you first start to realize?"

Sam twisted her lips as she thought. "I realized I was bisexual first, though I sort of realized that in high school—"

"Really? You never said."

"I didn't really know the name for it and...well, I wasn't sure how my girlfriend would react if she thought I was also attracted to men."

"Fair, I suppose," Jess admitted. "Do you have a ten?"

"Go fish." Sam shuffled her cards absently. "I think I was also afraid of being different. Everyone expected us to graduate and get married—"

"They expected I'd get pregnant and drop out."

Sam tapped the edge of the cards against her bottom lip as she softly laughed. "True. But my point still stands. I was scared to go against the grain. And most of all, I was scared I'd be rejected by the people I loved."

"I wouldn't have."

Sam smiled sweetly. "I know. Do you have a Jack?"

Jess huffed and handed over the card. "When did you realize you were a woman?"

"Part of me always knew something wasn't right, but I had the lightbulb moment when I went to my first drag show. Until then I didn't really think dressing like a woman was okay, but it looked right." Sam shoved a Cheeto in her mouth and washed it down with a sip of her drink. "I was too shy to talk to anyone at first, but Ben and Misty helped me drum up some courage, and by that, I mean Misty dragged me over to meet people."

"Did she know them?"

"Some. Do you have a six?"

"Go fish." Jess leaned against the pillows and stretched out her legs. "Are Ben and Misty...?"

"They're swingers."

"Not what I thought you were going to say, but yeah, that makes sense."

Sam opened her mouth, hesitating for a moment while her eyes flicked away from Jess. "I've sometimes...what I mean is, sometimes we've..."

"Fucked?"

Sam nodded.

"Nothing wrong with that."

"Really? It doesn't bother you?"

Jess shook her head. "Not at all. I can't really judge you for things I've done. Married couples love unicorns. Not that, Ben and Misty ever considered you one, but I've been one a few times."

"No, they don't. We care for each other; the sex is just a bonus. Whose turn is it again?"

"Mine, I think," Jess stared down at her cards. "I'm glad you had people to care for you. I just wish I had been here too, but I can't really blame anyone but myself for that."

Sam reached for Jess' hand and brushed her thumb over Jess' knuckles. "Things happen, Jess. No need to beat ourselves up over it. We're here now. Together."

Jess raised their hands to her mouth. "Thank you. Do you have a seven?"

Sam won three hands to Jess' two. They laid beside each other, cards and snacks cleared away and wine coolers empty, with shoulders touching. They had blown out the candles and let the shadows play on the ceiling, spurred on by the swirling gray clouds outside. A branch thwacked against the side of the house but neither jumped.

"Was it scary taking the hormones?" Jess whispered, her fingers trailing up and down Sam's wrist.

"At first. Even though the doctor explained it to me I was still terrified I was making a terrible choice. That I would regret it." Sam intertwined their fingers to still Jess' hand. "I noticed parts of my body started to grow softer. My face, my chest, my thighs. Subtle changes no one else but me noticed at first, but it was like breathing for the first time. It felt right. Finally. I looked in the mirror and I didn't dislike what I was seeing."

"Did you...have you done any surgery?"

Sam shook her head. "I briefly considered implants, I thought a bigger bust size would make me feel more like a woman, but I like my breast size."

"What about the other?"

"You mean my dick?"

"Yeah, that."

Sam muffled her laugh with her hand. "Still have it."

"Keeping it?"

"So far." Sam curled their intertwined hands towards her chest. "It's hard to explain, but I don't feel like less of a woman for it, and I just don't think I want to do the surgery for something that doesn't make me feel bad."

"I don't think you're less of a woman," Jess murmured, sidling closer to kiss a bare sliver of skin on Sam's shoulder.

Sam turned her head and kissed Jess' forehead. "Thanks."

They stayed like that. Close—breaths away from being entwined together—and lying still in the gentle darkness. Jess wondered if Sam had fallen asleep from how quietly she laid there.

"Remember the summer before junior year?" Jess whispered just in case Sam was asleep.

"Which part?"

"The week before school started up again and we skipped church to drive out to the beach and spend the day at the boardwalk."

"I remember. I still have tokens you never used in my glove box."

Jess turned on her side. "And on the way home you pulled down that dirt road on the other side of the field—"

"And we had the most awkward, fumbly sex ever." Sam chuckled, turning to face Jess. "I remember that too. I thought you were disappointed until you said, 'you know what would be funny,' right before carving a notch on my dashboard, and then asked to make another."

She grinned. "What can I say? I liked awkward and fumbly."

Sam scoffed.

"I mean it," Jess said. "I always felt loved and safe with you. No one else made me feel that way."

Sheets whispered as Sam closed the distance. Her lips lingered inches from Jess'. Fingers curled under Jess' chin and Sam's thumb brushed

Jess' bottom lip. So close. All Jess had to do was lean in while her heart clawed its way into her throat.

"It might disappoint you that I'm not so awkward anymore," Sam murmured.

"However will I survive," Jess teased, dragging their entwined hands down between her breasts and over her stomach.

Sam sucked in a shaky breath as her fingers brushed the damp curls between Jess' legs. "I might not survive."

"And this is why I chose the granny dress."

"Good choice," was all Sam said before crushing them together, kissing Jess fervently as if this were a dream. That they would wake up, cities and time stretched between them, alone in their own beds.

Warm air caressed Jess' skin as the dress was bunched around her waist in a tangle of fabric—the neckline shoved under her breasts and the hem rucked up around her hips. Sam's calloused fingers teased her open. Pliant. Swallowing every whimper until her mouth left Jess', kissing the freckles that sprinkled across Jess' collarbone and dipped down the valley between her breasts. Jess pressed her lips together, failing to keep her gasps quiet the moment Sam settled between her legs.

No, not awkward anymore.

She turned her head, pressing her mouth against her shoulder to keep quiet, gaze focused on the bottom of the stairs. Darkness gathered there. Wispy. Undulating. Tendrils like long, thin fingers stretched across the floor. Coming closer and closer to where she lay as if they wanted to touch her too. She didn't see eyes, but she felt them. Burning into her. Flaying her open. Judging her.

Slut.

Girls like that deserve what's coming to them.

Come on, sweetheart, it wasn't really that bad, was it?

Jess squeezed her eyes shut. She pressed her hand to mouth to keep her scream inside. The darkness, the voices, they weren't real. Sam was real. Mouth hot and wet and suckling Jess' clit with her perfect lips. Fingers eagerly aiding in unraveling Jess thread by thread.

That was real. Wanted. Jess just had to block out everything else. Every unworthy thought and memory that tried to claw its way into her brain, trying to ruin something so wonderful.

Jess' eyes snapped open and met the yellow eyes of her spectral watcher. The one that wasn't real. Couldn't be real. That was more defined than before. More like a man with loose clothing. Or was it skin? Hanging from blackened bones. Shadows wriggled like wet worms, black wispy bodies dropping to the floor with a wet plop that only Jess heard, and crawling back up the dark corpse.

It reached for her. Bony fingers trembling as shaky feet carried it forward. Her breath quickened, heart thudding against her sternum. Tears pricked her eyes.

Not real. Not real.

Cold caressed her cheek and followed the trail Sam had made, stopping in between her breasts. The shadow leaned down, dropping fat, cold worms onto Jess' cheeks like tears, perfect white teeth growing closer to the hand that covered her mouth.

Threads snapped. Jess ground her palm against her lips, containing her wail as her body spasmed and her eyes rolled back into her head. Warmth moved up. Replaced the cold. Sam peeled Jess' hand away from her mouth and kissed her, lips wet and tongue plunging into Jess' mouth so she could taste herself.

Heat grew. Scorched her skin. Anger flashed through her. Not hers. *Not real.* She banished the shadow back where it came. Back to the dark corner of her mind. Where it couldn't bother her or Sam. The voices silenced into submission with each thrust of Sam's hips and the soft endearments she breathed into Jess' ear. Jess clung to Sam. Terrified of letting go.

Real. Real.

Sam didn't know what woke her. The winds still whipped around the house but not as severe as before. Leaves rustled with every gust. Sam was used to all of those sounds. She blinked up at the ceiling and listened for what might have woken her.

Drip, drip, drip.

A leak? Sam slowly sat up, ears straining for the direction of the dripping. It wasn't a consistent noise. She heard it close, then far, then not at all for a few seconds and then heard it constantly for a minute. A sound that moved through the house. Was someone walking? Aveline?

Sam turned to wake up Jess but the bed beside her was empty. She didn't think. Didn't hesitate. The thin sheet landed on the floor in a rumpled heap. Sam stalked out of the living room, eyes darting around for the doors first, making sure they were all closed up tight and Jess hadn't walked outside into the storm.

A dark figure knelt in the open pantry, whispering words Sam couldn't make out. She reached for the flashlight they had left on the kitchen table. Soft white light danced across the floors and landed on the bottom of Jess' foot.

"Jess?"

She had crawled into the pantry, feet sticking out of the doorway and her shoulders hunched under the bottom shelf. Soft scratching came from inside. Sam crouched down and gently touched Jess' shoulder, but Jess didn't stop scratching at the stained wall. Light illuminated the brown spots that had grown larger since Sam had looked at them a few days ago. The edges seeped together, forming a shapeless blob.

"Jess, you're sleepwalking, baby," Sam whispered, brushing her fingers through Jess' hair. "Come back to bed."

"Under the house. In the pond," Jess mumbled.

Sam wrapped her arm around Jess' middle and slowly coaxed her into standing. Jess' eyes were half-lidded. Empty. Lost in whatever dream that had prompted her to drag herself out of bed. Sam walked her back to the couch and gently tucked her back in, rescuing the sheet from the floor and covering Jess up.

Quiet footsteps padded across the linoleum as Sam closed the pantry door and carefully slid the dining chairs in front of the side door and the front door. While Jess could probably move them if she got up again, Sam was likely to hear the screeching of the wood across the floor.

"What's wrong?" Jess softly croaked when Sam climbed back into the bed.

"Just checking things. Go back to sleep, baby."

"M'kay."

Sam carefully tucked Jess into her side, arm tight around her back, and rested her chin on top of Jess' head. The sleepwalking scared her. What if Jess walked into the pond and drowned? Or walked into the road and was hit by a car?

Maybe I should stay over more? Make sure she's safe.

Would Jess even want that?

Sleep finally claimed Sam once more, but as she balanced on the cusp of falling into the soft, dark void, she realized the dripping had stopped once she found Jess.

Chapter 8

CAR DOORS SLAMMED AND Jess watched from the rocking chair as Celia herded two boys roughly the same height up the gravel driveway, her daughter sitting on her hip with tiny arms wrapped around her mother's neck. Celia paused when she noticed Jess on the front porch and offered a small wave, her mouth pinched in an anxious smile. Jess wasn't sure why Celia might be anxious—Jess had already promised a truce while the kids were present—until Celia's husband closed the trunk of their car, his hands full of groceries bag.

Jess had never received an invite to the wedding. Hell, she hadn't even known Celia was getting married until it was a done deal. Jess had never met him, spoken with him, or even seen a picture of him. But as he walked up the driveway behind his wide-eyed children, Jess realized the real reason why Celia hadn't wanted to move back here to take care of Momma.

If Jess were to ask anyone in town, they would loudly proclaim they were not racist and they loved everybody equally no matter how their track record spoke against that proclamation. That wouldn't have stopped the stares if Celia moved back to town with her husband—a six-foot, broad-shouldered, dark-skinned black man—and their very obviously mixed children.

The boys stopped at the porch steps, both wearing matching shorts and a plain t-shirt but in different colors and small backpacks hanging from their backs. They looked up to their mother and waited for her to tell them that this person they didn't know was okay. *Safe.*

"Hey, Jess," Celia said, a sliver of fear making her voice tremble slightly. "Meet your nephews and niece. Boys meet your Auntie Jess."

Jess crouched down in front of the boys. One wore red while the other wore green. Dark eyes regarded her shyly as she held out her hand for each of them. The one wearing red grasped her fingers first with a wisp of a smile.

"That's Connor, he's the oldest," Celia said, voice awash with relief. "Jack Jr isn't much for shaking hands or touching in general unless he wants to."

"Hello," Jess said, offering a smile of her own.

"Hi," Connor mumbled.

Jack Jr didn't say anything, but he gave Jess a soft nod as if acknowledging her, his hands shoved into his pockets. That was good enough for her. Jess straightened, knees popping, and she nodded at who had to be Abby.

"Hello, Abby," she said.

The little girl peeked at Jess before turning her face back into Celia's neck, pink and white beads in her hair knocking together, and Celia chuckled. "She's a bit shy too." She patted her husband on the arm. "And this is Jake."

Jake smiled—a large genuine smile that Jess didn't expect because she imagined Celia told him everything and had thought he wouldn't like her at all given the tense relationship between his wife and her sister—and nodded. "Nice to finally meet you, Jess. I'd shake your hand but got my hands full." He held up the bags of groceries.

"Ah, sorry." Jess opened the screen door. "Why don't you come on in. Grandma's been waiting to see you. And the kitchen's on the left."

"Thanks," Jake said, flashing another smile as he walked past her, ushering the boys into the house with him.

Celia hesitated. "How's Momma today?"

"Good day. Mind is mostly clear, and she only cussed at me once so far." Jess grinned while Celia winced and carried Abby inside.

Whatever trepidation the kids had around Jess they didn't have the same with her mother. All three sat in the living room with Aveline and chatted her ears off. Not that Momma seemed to mind, her lips curved in a soft smile. Jess watched them from where she sat at the dining table, fingers tapping her coffee cup.

"When is Sam coming over?" Celia asked while helping her husband put the cold groceries away in the fridge.

Jess softly cleared her throat. "About, Sam, I wanted to..."

"You don't have to worry. I already know," Celia said. "I knew before, but I didn't want to say anything until Sam told you herself."

"Can't even be mad at that really," Jess sipped her cold coffee and wrinkled her nose. "I preferred hearing it from her. But to answer your question, Sam and her parents should be here in about an hour. Keith is bringing the grill since you said you wanted to grill out and we don't have one anymore."

"Oh, shoot, I forgot we got rid of it already. Thanks." Celia opened the fridge and tentatively sniffed. "Why does it smell like egg?"

"I boiled and peeled eggs. Miss Juniper is going to show me how to make deviled eggs."

Celia blinked. "You boiled eggs?"

"That's what I said."

"Without setting the house on fire?"

"Ha ha." Jess rolled her eyes and crossed the kitchen to pour out her coffee and make a fresh pot. "I asked Miss Juniper to teach me how to cook. We started with eggs. I haven't burned them in days and only a little bit sticks to the pan now."

Celia wrapped the bags together and tossed them into the mesh sack hanging in the pantry. "Wow. I'm impressed."

"Don't make fun of me."

"I'm not." Celia slumped into Jess' empty chair. "I think it's great you're trying something new."

"Never too late to learn how to cook," Jake added, pulling out a chair beside Celia. "I thought she was kidding when she told me how bad you were."

Jess blew stray hair away from her face. "She wasn't. I was pretty awful, but I also didn't really care to try too hard."

She sat across from them while waiting for the coffee. Despite it being early afternoon, sleep clung to her mind. Dark circles carved a hollow space under her eyes. She desperately wanted to sleep but every time she tried, she had dreams or she walked. Thankfully, she had yet to walk out of the house but each time she woke up somewhere she wasn't supposed to be, it scared her. She couldn't tell Celia any of that.

"I found Momma's recipe tin. Some of the cards are in bad shape and I was going to copy them down." Jess leaned her elbows on the table. "Maybe even try making some of them eventually."

"I think that'd be great. Mind making a copy for me too?" Celia asked.

Jess nodded. "I can do that." She looked between them. "So, how did you two meet?"

Jake reached for Celia's hand and intertwined their fingers with a soft smile. "Celia worked the breakfast shift at The Scotch Bonnet on the beach and I worked overnights at the gas station down the road. I used to go there every morning."

"Two eggs, scrambled hard, country ham, and a side of biscuits and gravy. You'd always fall asleep in your eggs." Celia giggled, squeezing his hand.

"Took me months to work up the courage to ask for her number."

Jess couldn't help the smile tugging at her lips as her sister stared into her husband's eyes. Would she and Sam be like that years from now? Still as mushy and loving as they had always been? Jess hoped so. Though she doubted they could even get married if they wanted to. At least, not here.

"So..." Celia turned her attention back to Jess. "You and Sam."

"What about us?"

"Did you pick up where you left off?"

Jess shrugged. "I guess you could say that."

"God, you are such bad liar, Jess." Celia leaned into her husband. "You are absolutely seeing her again; I can tell by that twinkle in your eye."

Jess rolled her eyes. "I do not have a twinkle—"

"I don't know, looks a bit like a twinkle," Jake teased. "I'm glad I get to officially meet Sam. I've heard a lot of about the trouble y'all used to get up to."

"Trouble is one way to put it," Jess laughed and looked between them. Jake Jr wasn't in the living room anymore. "One of your kiddos has pulled a disappearing act."

Celia shot around in her chair. "Connor, where did your brother go?"

Connor shrugged.

Celia huffed and stood. "He couldn't have wandered far."

"I'll check upstairs," Jess offered, sliding out of her chair.

"Thanks."

Jess jogged up the stairs where Pawpaw's door stood wide open. Peering inside, she saw Jake Jr standing by the window with one hand pressed against the glass and the other pressed to his mouth. He was stock still. Didn't even turn his head as she walked into the freezing cold room.

"Hey, buddy," —Jess knelt beside him— "you shouldn't be in here."

"Pond," he muttered, tapping small fingers against the glass.

Jess nodded slowly. "Yeah, that's a pond. We can go swimming in a bit, but I think your momma would prefer if you stayed downstairs, okay?"

Jake Jr fit his thumb into his mouth, not sucking on it but looking as if he were gently chewing on it. "No swim."

"Well, you don't have to if you don't want to. We can play inside, or I can show you how to catch frogs and lightning bugs. Whatever you want to do."

"There's a man in the pond."

Jess peered down at the pond but only saw the still surface of the water. "Where?"

He leaned closer. "Under the water. He's stuck."

"Oh—"

"He deserves it."

Jess stood frozen at the window, staring down at the motionless pond while Jake Jr walked out of the room and back down the stairs. Nothing popped up from the water. Not a man or a beast. A shiver ran up her spine anyway, with her trying to chalk it up to him being a strange child but she just wasn't sure about things anymore.

"He was in Pawpaw's room," Jess said when she finally walked back down the stairs—the room shut tight in the hopes of deterring any of the children from going back in—and saw Jake Jr sitting with his siblings on the couch, quietly coloring in a book. "I think he was just curious."

Celia's mouth twitched. "Yeah, he is. We have to be careful though. He likes to wander and being so close to the water...well, we just want to be careful."

Jess poured herself a fresh cup of coffee. "He said something odd."

"He does that," Jake said, tapping the side of his cup. "Doctors think he's autistic."

"We don't know for sure yet, they're still running tests," Celia quickly added.

"I have a brother and a few uncles that are. I'm pretty sure he is," Jake said, voice tight.

Jess could tell they had argued about this before. Probably many, many times while waiting for an official diagnosis from a doctor. "Nothing wrong with being a little different," Jess said, pouring sugar into her coffee.

"It would be a lot different," Celia murmured. "Frankly, I'm not sure how to handle it."

Jake looked away, fingers tightening around the handle of his cup.

"He's your son. You'll figure it out," Jess said.

"Thank you for the *amazing* advice, Jess," Celia snapped.

Jess opened her mouth, but Jake softly cleared his throat. "I believe a truce was promised. Let's keep to that."

Familiar rumbling came from the end of the road and Jess set down her coffee up. "I think that's Sam and them. I'm gonna go help Keith unload the grill."

"I'll help too." Jake followed her outside, leaving Celia to stew at the table.

Sure enough, Jess saw Sam's familiar car working its way down the dirt road—worse off after the hurricane and the owner hadn't graded it yet to even it out—with the trailer hitched behind it. She waited on the porch steps.

"She means well," Jake said.

"Hm?"

"Celia."

Jess shrugged. "I guess."

"She just worries about everything. Dwells on the negative and drives herself up the wall."

"That's Celia. Always worrying. Always trying to fix things even when they're not broken yet," Jess muttered. "She keeps it up she's going to have a full head of gray hair in a few years."

Jake chuckled. "She's already plucked a few."

Jess muffled a burst of laughter against her fist.

"So, how are you, Jess? Really?" he asked.

"I'm doing fine."

"Are you?"

She threw him a side glance. "If this is an attempt at tricking me into opening up so you can tell Celia everything, you're doing a bad job."

He held up his hands. "No nefarious intentions here, promise. I just don't want you think no one cares about you out here. We do. Celia definitely does."

Jess didn't know what to say. It didn't change the anger Jess still held within her. Didn't fix things between her and her sister. What did it matter that Celia cared when she had shoved off the burden of taking care of their mother onto Jess?

"You don't have to tell me anything, but I do want you to know you can call us if you need help or just…someone to talk to. Okay?"

Sam pulled to a stop at the end of the driveway and Jess nodded at what Jake said, ready to leave it alone. "Thanks."

The scent of coconut and sand infiltrated Jess' nose as she buried her face in Sam's chest. Sam kissed the top of her head while Juniper and Keith climbed out of the cab. She vaguely heard them introduce themselves to Jake, but she wasn't paying attention.

"I like your other soap better," she grumbled. "The one that smells like mint."

Sam snorted. "Sorry, they were fresh out." She ran her fingers through Jess' hair. "Sorry we're late. Lily threw a fit."

Jess pulled back. "What about?"

"Well, she's grounded but she couldn't stay home by herself because Ma knew she would try to sneak off to her boyfriend's again." Sam nodded to the truck. "She's sulking."

Sitting in the middle of the back bench was a sullen teenager—black sunglasses hiding her eyes but not the downturn of her lips into a pout—with her arms crossed over chest. Lily was a near carbon copy of Sam and almost as tall. Wispy blond hair was pulled back into a ponytail, and she wore a tank top, blue swimsuit straps peeking out from underneath the yellow fabric.

Jess crossed her arms against the open window and leaned in. "Hey, Lily."

"Will you tell them they're being ridiculous, Jess?" Lil huffed. "You and Sam used to sneak around all the time and never got in trouble."

"Not entirely true—"

Lily pushed her glasses down the bridge of her nose and stared at Jess over thick black frames. "Please," she scoffed. "You were always sneaking out at night and during school and after church and—"

"Yeah, okay, okay, I get it." Jess waved her hand. "You're also the bonafide baby of the family so rules are different for you."

"It's because I'm a *girl*."

"More than likely," Jess agreed. "Who is the boyfriend anyway?"

"James," Sam answered in a tight voice.

Jess blew out a breath. "It's not because you're a girl, it's because you're dating an asshole."

"He isn't—"

Jess raised an eyebrow.

Lily rolled her eyes and slumped down in the seat. "There's another side to him."

"You're the only one who's seen it." Jess opened the door. "Now, I know you at least want to swim while you're here and I know you've missed me."

Lily's lips twitched. "Fine," she sighed. "I did miss you." She climbed out and wrapped her thin arms around Jess' neck, smelling strongly of cherry blossom body spray.

A full house produced a level of noise Jess hadn't heard in a long time. Kids played and adults drank. The kitchen door sat propped open—screen door keeping out droves of flies—while Keith and Jake walked in and out, sipping beer and warming up the grill. Jess at the table next to Juniper, cutting eggs and scraping out yolks. The hostility between her and Celia didn't exist with everyone else as a buffer, keeping the tone light.

This is what Jess had missed the most.

"Pretty nice, huh," Sam said as they sat on the muddy bank, watching the kids and Lily splash around in the water. Jake Jr sat with her, absently braiding blades of grass together.

Jess leaned into Sam. "Yes."

Sam dragged her fingers down Jess' spine, making her shiver. "I've missed this."

"Which part?"

Sam kissed her cheek. "All of it."

"Well, then," —Jess turned her head to brush her lips against Sam's— "maybe we should do this more often."

Lily made an exaggerated gagging sound.

Jess leaned away with a laugh. "Later then."

Sam grasped her hand. "It's a date."

"Food's almost ready!" Celia called from the porch. "Come get cleaned up."

Jess stood as the kids got out of the water but lingered on the bank, reluctant to stop swimming so soon. She knew that feeling. Momma used to call her a fish. Always swimming any chance she could. Taking long baths until her fingers were pruny.

A flash in the water caught her attention. She squinted thinking it was possibly a snake, but she didn't see anything slithering across the surface of the water. Jess took a tentative step into the water.

"Jess?" Sam questioned.

"Thought I saw something," Jess called over her shoulder while moving her hands through the water as if that might help her see. "Think one of the kids might've dropped something."

"Do you see it?"

Grasses growing out of the silt tickled her feet as she walked. Scaly bodies slapped against her legs before darting away. Nothing out of the ordinary glinted in the muddy water.

Jess turned back. "No, there's not—"

Something snagged her ankle, pulling her under the surface. Water entered her mouth and up her nose as she coughed. Fingers scrambled to find solid ground and push herself back up. Pain shot through her knee as it scraped a rock. A hand wrapped around her arm and pulled her up, coughing and sputtering.

"Are you okay?" Sam asked, smacking Jess' upper back.

"Yeah," she choked out between coughs. "I just slipped, that's all."

"Wow, Jess, when did you become a clutz?" Lily deadpanned from the shore.

"Shut up, Lily," Sam snapped. "Go in the house and help Momma if you're gonna be a jerk."

Lily's face turned bright red, and she turned on her heel to stomp up to the house with the other kids following her like confused little ducklings. Sam kept a hold of Jess until they were out of the water.

"You sure you're okay?"

Jess nodded. "I'm fine. Just got snagged by some grass I think."

"You're bleeding," Sam said, crouching down to look at Jess' knee. "Come on, let's go up to the house and I'll clean that for you."

Celia got the kids through the shower downstairs while Jess went upstairs to rinse off in the shower. An endeavor that took longer than normal when Sam joined her, rinsing murky water from her hair and kissing her until the water ran cold. If anyone noticed, and they probably did, they said nothing when Jess joined them once more with antibiotic gel slathered onto her knee and Sam holding her hand.

The night passed with good food, good drink, and more laughing than Jess had done in a while. She didn't want it to end.

Warmth and wet coated her skin, cloying each breath that entered her lungs. Jess woke with a gasp, eyes crusted shut and keeping her locked into darkness, her fingers pushing through cold damp. Breaths squeezed out of her lungs. Panic rose into her throat. Jess freed her fingers from muck and clawed at her eyes.

She blinked up at old wood joists, covered in spreading water spots. Freckled rot burrowing through the wood reminded her of the dark spots growing in the pantry. Bigger and bigger each day.

A whimper escaped her lips.

The wood creaked above her. Footsteps walking around in the house she laid under. Voices trickled down through the gaps in the wooden boards. She recognized Sam's voice among them.

"I'm here," she wanted to say. Wanted to scream for them.

Would they even hear her?

Jess rolled over onto her stomach. Sparse patches of weeds grew in the crawlspace. A few cans with labels long since faded sat crushed near the entrance as if someone had just thrown them inside instead of throwing them away or they had blown in during a storm. Rusted chains attached to columns of old brick twisted like snakes in the mud. With a soft cry, she crawled on her elbows to the sunlit opening. Fingers grasped warm brick. Grass came away in her hands. Dirt pushed underneath her fingernails. She squirmed through the opening and landed on her belly in the yard.

Soft footsteps stopped in front of her.

Jess looked up at Jake Jr clutching a bedraggled teddy bear to his chest. He didn't look afraid of finding her like this, his eyes filled with pity more than fear. Hot tears filled hers. They dripped down her face. Splattered onto the ground.

"She's all alone down there," Jake Jr said, holding out his hand.

Jess sucked in a shaky breath and took her nephew's hand. The edges of her vision were hazy. Dreamlike. Perhaps she was dreaming this too. Her legs shook. He led her around the house as if she might've forgotten how to enter it and she followed him onto the porch.

Lively voices died immediately when she stepped into the kitchen. All eyes were on her. So many eyes. All judging or worried. Making her more sick than she already felt.

"Oh my God, Jess," Celia set her coffee cup down onto the table before she dropped it.

"What on earth happened?" Juniper asked before anyone else could. "You are covered in mud, hun'."

"W-went for a walk and I tripped," Jess croaked.

"Wow, Jess," Lily said, but her voice lacked the edge of teenager sarcasm she normally had. "You've been awfully clumsy lately."

Jess tried to laugh but it was wrong. Stilted. Scared. "I should go wash up. I'll be back."

The banister groaned as she pulled herself up the stairs, her knees barely able to hold herself up. She slammed the bathroom door shut and climbed into the tub before her legs gave out. Water turned the mud caked to her body into a thick slurry, staining the porcelain and snaking down the drain.

Not even the warm water could stop her trembling.

Jess hugged her knees to her chest and bit back sobs.

The door softly creaked open and closed again. A soft shadow waited on the other side of the yellowing curtain, standing for a heartbeat, two heartbeats, and then kneeling beside the tub.

"Where did you wake up?" Sam asked, her voice low as if loud sounds might shatter Jess.

"Under the house," she whispered, fresh tears springing to her eyes.

Sam let out a shaky breath much like the one Jess did when she freed herself from the crawlspace. "Shit, baby."

"I don't know what's happening to me," Jess nearly sobbed. She wouldn't be able to hold them in much longer as her chest heaved, ready to make her either cry or vomit or both.

"I'm going to open the curtain, okay?"

"Okay."

Sam pulled the curtain back. Her eyes darted over Jess' huddled form. Searching for injuries maybe. Or some other physical sign that Jess was absolutely losing it. When she didn't see anything, she leaned closer and wiped streaks of dirt from Jess' face to cup her cheek.

"Has it ever been this bad?" Sam asked.

Jess shook her head.

Sam looked away, her lips thinned into a line and her brow furrowed. "I think...I think I should move in for a bit. Stay with you, at least at night." She looked back at Jess. "How does that sound?"

"I don't want to be a burden," she mumbled.

Sam leaned close and touched her forehead to Jess', not caring about the streaks of dirt marring her skin. "Making sure you're safe isn't a burden. It doesn't have to be permanent if you don't want it to be, but just until this stops."

"What if it never stops?"

Sam kissed her forehead. "We will figure it out. I won't leave you to deal with this by yourself."

The dam broke. Jess leaned into Sam, fingers grasping the edge of the porcelain tub, while sobs wracked her body.

What was happening to her?

Chapter 9

GREEN LIGHT FLICKERED FROM the baby monitor as it teetered on the edge of sink. Aveline's soft breaths crackled through, even and steady as if she had dozed off while Jess scrambled to get ready. Holding the corner of her eyelid taut, she swiped the black pencil over her lash line and carefully smudged the liner with her forefinger. Jess leaned back and looked at herself in the mirror wondering if the makeup was too much for the county fair. In the city, she was always heavy handed, putting on a mask as much as she was dressing herself up.

She leaned away too fast, her arm knocking the sink. The baby monitor clattered to the ground and knocked the back off. Batteries rolled across the floor.

"Fuck."

Jess swept up the batteries and popped them back into the monitor, flicking the switch with her thumb. Another curse rolled off her tongue when the light didn't immediately turn back on. She smacked it against her palm. The light flickered between red and green. A soft noise came through. Jess held it to her ear, waiting to hear her mother breathing.

A staticky soft cry wailed in her ear. Jess poked her head out the door and listened for the same sound from Momma but heard nothing but the drone of the TV downstairs. Another cry. A baby crying. Distant. Sad. Jess' stomach flipped. It had to be interference. Another baby monitor close by. She smacked it against her hand again.

The sound stopped.

Jess let out a breath and set down the monitor, shaking hand picking up the pencil to finish her makeup. She swiped red lipstick across her lips and rubbed them together.

The front door opened. Sam's voice traveled up the stairs as she greeted Aveline. Jess ran from the bathroom to her room, eyeing the pile of outfits she had already rejected but she didn't have any more options. A pale-yellow dress with sunflowers—one she had picked out from the thrift store—was the winner. The skirt skimmed her knees. Fabric brushed the irritated cut on her knee.

She leaned down and poked at the angry red slash. While it had been over a week since she cut her knee in the pond, the cut hadn't gone away. The first few nights had been fine. Then Jess started to pick and scratch. She hardly knew she was doing it until blood coated her fingers.

"Hey," Sam said, pausing in the doorway. "You look great."

Jess did a turn. "It's not too much?"

"I would've picked pink lipstick instead of red," Sam teased.

Jess stuck out her tongue.

"Careful, Jess. Wouldn't want to start something you can't finish."

Heat gathered in her belly but before she could come up with a sexy retort, Sam's gaze moved lower and locked on Jess' knee.

"Were you picking at it again?" Sam asked, crossing her arms under her chest.

Jess tried to tug the hem over the cut as if Sam would forget about it. "It itched."

"It's going to itch while it's healing," Sam sighed. "But you have to leave it alone. We can wrap it so you won't keep opening it up."

"It's not a big deal."

Sam pursed her lips. "Please leave it be, Jess. Infections can get bad if we're not careful."

Jess huffed. "Okay, mom."

"What are you a teenager?" Sam shook her head. "I'm going to run through the shower. Then we can go."

"Fine."

Sam tapped the door frame before walking back in the hall to the bathroom. "Oh, and since you want to call me mom, why don't you pick up your clothes," she called back and snickered.

Jess rolled her eyes. "Cute."

Despite the attitude, Jess couldn't be happier that Sam had moved in. They had cleared out a drawer and a space in Jess' closet for some of Sam's clothes and had a basket underneath the sink with Sam's toiletries. Officially, Sam was sleeping in Celia's old bed, but more often than not, Sam climbed into Jess' small bed. Sometimes sleeping, sometimes not. While they could push the beds together, Jess liked the nostalgic feeling of Sam sneaking into her bed.

Telling her to put away her clothes had been a joke, but Jess still took a moment to clean off her bed and put everything back where it belonged. She grabbed the baby monitor and carried it downstairs to hand off the responsibility to Juniper.

"Well don't you look lovely tonight, Jess," Miss Juniper said while sitting on the couch, a romance novel in her lap.

Momma cut her eyes at Jess but didn't say anything. She was having one of her bad days. While at the breakfast table she had gone so far as to throw her eggs onto the floor and almost dump her coffee in her lap. Thankfully, Sam had already gone to work and didn't see Jess trying to clean up the mess while fighting back tears. The day had not gotten better from there.

Jess set the baby monitor down onto the table and plopped onto the couch. "You don't think it's too much?"

"For you? No."

Momma scoffed under her breath but otherwise remained quiet.

"It's been a while since I've gone out," Jess admitted. "Though going to the fair is different than going out to the club."

"A bit less dancing unless you like square dancing," Juniper agreed.

"I can't remember the last time I square danced," Jess said. What she didn't say was that she had learned how to square dance at one of those backwoods country bars they used to sneak to as teenagers.

"Don't ask me to teach you; I don't remember either," Sam teased, walking into the living room all pink and scrubbed clean of grease and machine oil. She wore denim shorts—the ones that didn't have any rips in them—and a pink-checked button up over a white tank top. Her blond hair was pulled back into a high ponytail. Pink gloss gave her lips a sheen in the light.

"Ready?" Sam asked, holding out her hand.

Jess grasped the hand that helped her off the couch. "Ready."

"We won't be out too late—"

Juniper waved away Sam's words. "Lord knows, it wouldn't hurt you kids to stay out late for once. I'll be just fine with Miss Beverly Jenkins." She held up her book and winked. "And don't worry, I'll make sure Miss Aveline and I don't get too wild."

The corner of Momma's mouth twitched.

Bugs chittered and chirped their shrill tones in the evening air that clung to Jess' skin like a damp towel. She already felt her eyeliner smear as sweat oozed from her pores. By the time the night was over, Sam might mistake her for a raccoon.

Sam hummed as they drove down main street and towards the highway. The fair was held in the same place every year. Surrounding towns flocked to the barren patch of field—sucked dry of nutrients after planting the same crop year after year—where even grass struggled to take hold. She hoped the mix of people would prevent her from seeing too many townsfolk. She didn't want anything to ruin their date.

"When's the last time you went?" Jess asked to quell the silence.

"Last year. I chaperoned Lily and her friends, and I can't tell you how thrilled she was about that," Sam said, dripping sarcasm. "But she hasn't been making the best decisions lately."

"And we did?"

Sam shrugged. "We were different. We kept each other from going overboard. Lily's friends are...destructive on a level we weren't."

"I don't know. Teenage girls trying to destroy themselves before life does it for them sounds about right to me," Jess murmured, leaning her head against the window and watching the trees bend.

"And I didn't let you. I won't let Lily either if I can help it."

"You can't watch her forever."

"I know."

Jess slid towards the center of the seat and leaned her head on Sam's shoulder. "She'll be okay, even if she makes fucked up choices now. That's what kids do. They push boundaries and make god-awful decisions. You'll have to let her grow from them."

Sam let go of the wheel to squeeze Jess' thigh. "I will. I just don't want her to get hurt. And dating the Reverend's son—who is closer to our age need I remind you—will get her hurt."

"We both know that, but if you push too hard, you'll push her towards him instead of away. All you can do is wait and hope she realizes that before it's too late."

Sam's fingers tightened on the wheel. "I hate that option."

"I know." Jess kissed her cheek. "But it's the only one that gives her a safety net when things go to shit."

The parking lot was as full as Jess had hoped it would be. Cars she didn't recognize parked in neat little rows. The chances of them running into folks from town dwindled with each row Sam crawled down until she found a space near the tree line all the way in the back. Jess didn't mind the walk to the brightly lit entrance, her hand intertwined with Sam's and a spring in her step.

Loud music made her ears ring. People chattered and little kids screamed as they rode the kiddie coaster—a coaster Jess and friends used to ride when high because it was fun and laidback. The sweet smell of fried funnel cake tickled her nose. She wouldn't be leaving without having at least one, maybe two if she wanted to treat herself.

Sam let Jess lead, a smile tugging at her lips as Jess nearly raced to The Scrambler—a ride best done on an empty stomach. Barely anyone spared Sam a second glance. Out here they were a pair of nobodies. Just yokels from another town that no one else gave a damn about.

Sweet and tart iced tea with lemonade wet her whistle while Sam tried her hand at darts. Jess had rolled her eyes at the way Sam said, "I can try my hand at it if you want," as if Sam wasn't annoyingly good at hitting her targets. But she always let Jess pick out the prize, so it didn't annoy Jess too much.

"Hungry yet?" Sam asked, as they walked amongst the food stands.

Jess tucked the giant pink teddy bear with heart-shaped purple eyes under her arm and nodded.

"The usual?"

"Do you even remember the usual?" Jess scoffed.

Sam rolled her eyes. "You want a cheeseburger, extra pickles and ketchup, cheese fries, a corn dog, and funnel cake. You want the same thing every year at the fair. Trust me, I didn't forget."

"I was just wondering. Maybe my tastes had changed."

"Not where food is concerned. You've always liked the same things." Sam chuckled. "Now, why don't you go find a table and I'll be right there."

"You don't need help?"

Sam lovingly cut her eyes at Jess for daring to question Sam's ability to carry everything on her own.

"Okay, okay," Jess said. "I'll go."

She found a picnic table tucked beside a stand selling slushies. Jess used to love those too until she poured too much vodka into one and became violently ill. Ever since then the sticky sweet taste of cherry syrup made her gag. She didn't want to try any of the other flavors just in case they did the same. The pink bear kept her company on the bench while she waited, watching Sam stand in line.

Men watched too. They let their eyes linger on Sam, gazes trailing down to gawk at the way Sam's jeans hugged her ass. They elbowed each other. Jess recognized their frenzied movements, trying to push one or the other to approach Sam first as if one getting her number were a win for all of them. Until, of course, they realized Sam wasn't their ideal woman.

They would punish her for it. That's what they did.

Anger curled in her stomach. Acid clawed up her throat. She wished she could grow claws. Slash their skin to ribbons, feeding the starving ground with their blood. Jess wanted to hurt them before they could hurt someone else.

"Jess, honey?" Sam stood beside the table holding a small stack of foam containers. "Are you okay?"

Jess tore her eyes away from the group, forcing herself to look away from the way they leered at Sam and now her. One reached down and adjusted himself.

"I'm fine," she forced out and smiled.

Sam sat down across from her. "I don't believe you."

She shrugged. "I just didn't like how they were looking at you."

"Was it jealousy or...?" Sam raised a brow.

"If they weren't so disgusting, maybe."

"Ah." Sam pushed a box towards Jess. "I'll admit. I'm still not used to how some guys will look at me, even though I know who I am would disgust them."

"I'd say welcome to being a woman, but it's such a shitty thing. Definitely one thing that is just as bad in the city as it was at home." Jess sipped the pink lemonade Sam had brought but it only added to the bubbling pit of acid in her belly.

"Don't worry too much about it right now. Let's just have a nice time."

Jess nodded.

Thick cheese coated perfectly fried crinkle cut fries. The corndog audibly crunched as she bit into it. Jess leaned over the tray as ketchup escaped the cheesy and greasy burger. But nothing compared to the powdered sugar perfection of funnel cake. Sam had bought Jess her own, knowing damn well that Jess would share anything else if asked, but she never shared funnel cake.

While Sam had told Jess not to worry about it, Jess couldn't help but watch as the group of men sat at a close table. Especially when their eyes strayed to Jess. A few made eye contact but quickly looked away when Jess glared at them.

She couldn't get away from them fast enough as she cleaned up their trash and carried it to the trash cans beside the stands. With a hand on the small of Jess' back, Sam navigated them past the tables.

"Hey!"

Jess tensed instantly, her hands curling into fists.

"What?" Sam said over her shoulder.

A sandy-haired man with brown eyes grinned. "You ladies look you could use some company."

"You're mistaken," Jess snapped.

The man held up his hands, the grin still plastered onto his face. "No need to be hostile. We're just looking for some fun."

"Appreciate the offer, but we'll have plenty of fun on our own," Sam said, her voice only slightly shaky.

"Yeah? Any chance we could watch?" Another leered at them while the table erupted in laughter.

Anger returned. A festering infection that tunneled its way through her. Jess' hands shook. If Sam hadn't felt Jess' trembling and immediately wrapped her arm around Jess' waist, Jess would've swung already until bone crunched under her fists.

"I don't think y'all want any of that," an annoyingly familiar voice called out over the laughter and dashed Jess' hopes of them going unrecognized for the night.

"Fuck," Sam swore by Jess' ear.

James—the Reverend's son in all of his irritating glory—sauntered close with Lily following behind him, eyes wide with fear. For her own sister or her boyfriend, Jess wasn't sure. Perhaps this was it. The moment Lily saw that her adult boyfriend was nothing but a predatory piece of shit. Better now than when he starts hitting her.

"You think it's a woman because it knows how to put on lipstick and stuff its shirt," James sneered, voice already thick with alcohol and slurring words. "Then you get it home and you're the one getting fucked."

Lily grasped his arm. "James, please—"

"I'm just warning these good people, Lily!" he exploded, shaking her off until she stumbled back. "Don't want them getting raped by some tranny."

Jess shifted and Sam's arm tightened around her, but Sam was shaking too.

The sandy-haired man's lip curled in disgust. "Fucking freak," he spat at Sam's feet, the thick gob landing on Jess' boot instead. "And you weren't going to tell us. Just gonna wait until we took you home, huh?"

"You weren't taking anyone home," Jess hissed.

"And what about you, bitch? You gotta dick too?" He stood. "Maybe we oughtta check."

"Nah, Jess is all woman, aren't you sweetheart?" James snickered. "She'll open her legs if you ask nicely enough. Won't you, Jess?"

Sam stepped back, dragging Jess with her. "We're leaving."

James called something after them, but Jess couldn't hear over the blood pounding in her ears. They made it back to the entrance, all sense of fun vanished in an instant. Jess wanted to hit something. She wanted to go home. She wanted blood in her teeth.

"I need you to climb in quickly from the driver's side," Sam murmured over the roaring. "They're right behind us. I don't want to give them a chance."

Let them come. Let them try.

"Where are you going?" one of them taunted.

"We just want to have a little fun," another added.

Sam opened the door, but she wasn't fast enough. Fingers curled in her hair and yanked her away from Jess. She didn't even have time to draw breath before a meaty fist sank into her gut. Cheers erupted as Sam doubled over.

"Leave her alone!" Jess shrieked, rushing at the sandy-haired man.

He turned with a chuckle and shoved her against the open door. "Wait your turn, bitch. We'll have plenty of time for you."

Pain exploded in her shoulder as it hit the hard steering wheel. She stumbled, grasping the step to steady herself. Another wet hit came from behind her. Sam groaned. Something shiny called to Jess from under the seat. Her fingers curled around the heavy wrench. She didn't think. Didn't have to. The man cocked back his fist to swing again, blood from Sam's lip stained his knuckles, and Jess swung. A crack thundered in the parking lot and the man screamed, reaching for his elbow.

She wasn't satisfied.

The second hit cost him teeth. He spat the pearly whites on the grass, blood spraying across Jess' dress and the poor car parked beside the truck. With a cry, he stumbled away from her and tripped over his own feet. Heat of a different kind gathered in her belly at the fear in his eyes. At the way he whimpered and crab-walked away from her so she wouldn't hit him again.

Vomit sprayed from his mouth as the wrench smashed into his knee. No one helped him. His friends watched in horror, backing away as Jess drew closer. She soaked in the fear. They were afraid of *her*.

Good.

"Enough, Jess," Sam's voice was a whisper amidst the noise.

Was it enough? She wasn't sure.

"Get the fucking wrench from her!" James hollered, face red and lips flecked with spit. "She's just some bitch."

"A crazy fucking bitch," one of the other men said, shaking his head. "I'm out of here."

They ran like dogs with tails tucked between their legs. Well, except for the one who limped away while two of his friends held him up between them. James stayed with Lily's wrist in an iron grip to keep her from going to her sister.

Jess pointed the wrench at him. "Let her go."

"Drop the fucking wrench," he sneered.

She shrugged and let it drop. For James, she didn't need it. He was soft. Always hiding behind his father. Dodging consequences with the power of clergy. Jess didn't see his father. No shield for him to hide behind. She waited until he dropped Lily's wrist, wanting nothing more than to wipe the smug smirk off his face, and launched herself at him.

"What the f—"

Her knuckles split open, the pain barely registering, as her first punch glanced off his teeth. Blood splashed into his mouth while he yelled. She couldn't hear what he was saying. One punch and he was James, another and he was the Reverend, a third and she froze.

Garth's dark brown eyes looked up into hers. White teeth edged with yellow, one of his canines missing from a bar fight years ago, bared at her. With a yell, she cocked her first back once more and slammed it into Garth's wide nose. He just kept smiling.

Come on baby, it won't hurt so bad if you relax.

Do you like making me hit you?

Am I supposed to feel sorry for you after you tried to baby trap me?

Each phrase echoed in her head. Rang in her ears. He was lying on the ground eating her punches with a bloody smile and he was in her head. Taunting her. Vicious words encircling her throat like his meaty hands.

She'd wipe the smile off his face.

Another punch. Another splatter of blood. His. Hers. Didn't matter. She didn't feel anything but the white hot rage that finally blazed inside of her. Embroiling her insides. An unquenchable anger that she had held inside like a knife in the hand, waiting for the moment she slipped and sliced open her skin.

Pawpaw stared up at her. Black eyes sunken into sagging, wrinkled skin. Cracked lips framed a blood-filled mouth. He smiled.

You were always my favorite, Jessamine.

She screamed in his face.

A hand grasped her wrist. An arm snaked around her waist.

No! I'm not done!

"You have to stop," Sam's voice barely penetrated the roaring inferno. "Please, baby, you have to stop."

Jess was hoisted to her feet. The toes of her boots kicked up grass and dry soil as she tried to break out of Sam's hold, but Sam's arms wrapped around her tight—hands locking together under Jess' chest—and her chin resting on Jess' head. No matter how hard Jess tried to wriggle out of Sam's hold, she couldn't.

"Come back to me, Jess," Sam breathed in her ear.

"No, let me go!" Jess shrieked, fingers clawing at Sam's arm. "Let me go! I have to...I have to..."

James groaned on the ground, eyes swollen shut, nose crooked and red, lips split open and weeping blood onto his chin. Lily leaned over him, eyes wide and glassy. Her shoulders shook as she met Jess' eyes.

Did I do that? No. No. It wasn't him.

Jess doubled over, Sam following her, and screamed until her voice gave out.

Jess didn't speak a word as Sam turned down the road leading back into town. She curled herself into as close as a ball as she could get and crushed herself against the passenger door. Shaking shoulders told Sam she was probably crying or shivering from the shock.

The silence was too much but Sam didn't want to reach across and fiddle with the radio dial in case the movement upset Jess even more.

Sam had tried to get Lily to leave with them, but she had refused, wanting to be there when the deputies showed up so she could give her witness statement about a group of assholes jumping James—who wouldn't argue because he wouldn't want to admit he got beat up by one woman. While Lily could hardly look at Jess while Sam loaded Jess into the car and grabbed the bloody wrench from the ground, she wasn't going to throw Jess under the bus. Not for a problem James created. Sam just hoped this was enough to encourage her to dump him.

A muffled sob echoed in the quiet cab.

Sam pulled off onto an old road—a former driveway hidden in a cluster of woods that led to a house that no one had lived in for many years. No one would find them here. She wasn't ready to take them home yet. Not like this. Sam parked the car and slumped down in her seat.

An ugly red mark on her cheek throbbed, promising a large purple bruise that would get people asking questions. Mostly her parents.

And she would tell them the truth. They were the only ones she trusted with the truth, and it would die with them.

"I'm sorry," Jess whispered.

Sam let out a soft breath. "Jess—"

"I w-won't hurt you; I promise."

"Why would I think you'd hurt me?"

Jess didn't answer.

"Baby, why would I think you'd hurt me?" Sam repeated, keeping her voice soft.

"I didn't mean to. I-I didn't..."

"Jess, come here," Sam murmured. "Come here so I can hold you, sweetheart."

She didn't move at first. Seconds ticked into a minute before her limbs unfurled. Fingers moved like spiders across the bench seat as Jess turned her wide glassy eyes to Sam. Her bottom lip quivered. Fear shone bright in her eyes. For herself or for Sam, Sam wasn't sure. Jess slowly crawled across the seat, balking for a brief moment when Sam reached out for her, but allowed Sam to pull Jess into her lap. She straddled Sam's hips, entrapping herself between Sam and the steering wheel.

Sam brushed hair away from Jess' face and cradled her cheeks. "There you are," she whispered.

Shaky fingers brushed the swelling bruise on Sam's face. Jess choked back a sob. "I'm sorry."

"This isn't your fault—"

"I'm the one who wanted to go." Jess sniffed.

"This could've happened whether you were with me or not," Sam reassured, thumbs brushing Jess' cheekbones. "You can't take the blame for this. And who knows what would've happened if you weren't there."

"But I...I lost control. I hurt...I could've hurt you."

"No, you wouldn't have."

Jess' brow furrowed. "You don't know that."

"Baby," Sam crooned, hands moving back so she could tangle her fingers in Jess' hair and pulled her closer, lips hovering inches away. "I've always known the anger that lives in you, and what you're capable of."

Jess slowly shook her head, but she didn't speak.

Sam kept one hand in Jess' hair while the other brought Jess' bloody and torn knuckles to her lips. Dried blood flaked onto her mouth. "I know you, Jess, and I'm not scared of you."

"W-why?"

"Why, what?" Sam asked, kissing each and every one of Jess' fingers. "Why am I not scared of you?"

"Why would you still want me after that?"

"Because you were protecting me" Sam murmured, hands trailing down Jess' waist and over her hips. "Protecting us."

Jess leaned down and tucked her face in the crook of Sam's neck, warm breath sliding against Sam's jugular. "I liked it. I wanted to hurt them."

"I know."

"I'm a bad person."

Sam's fingers twisted in Jess' hair and she pulled her head back until Jess gasped, the fear in her eyes melting into desire. "Not a bad person."

"Then why did you stop me?" Jess challenged, the whimpering and whispering gone.

Good. Come back to me, baby.

Sam brushed her lips over Jess', pulling away when Jess tried to surge forward, and kept a firm grip on Jess' hair. "Because I don't want to be confined to conjugal visits when I want to fuck my girlfriend."

"Is that what I am?"

"That and every other thing you could think of."

Jess' eyes flashed. "And what if I don't think so."

"Then I'll go along with it, but tell me, baby," —Sam trailed up Jess' thigh, inching under the hem of Jess' skirt until her fingers brushed the damp fabric trapped between Jess' legs— "how many others would understand how wet you get after a fight?"

Jess shuddered. "Not fair—"

"Do you remember the first time? I do." Sam pulled Jess close, squashing the space between them into nothing, so Jess could feel the sincerity of Sam's words pressing against the thin fabric of her underwear. "You came so quickly on my fingers, and that still wasn't enough for you. I took every bit of your anger. Every scrape of your nails on my skin."

"Tell me why," Jess mumbled, eyes half-lidded.

"Because I love you." Sam rocked her hips until Jess sucked in a breath. "Every bit of you. Always have."

"Even though—"

"*Always*," Sam repeated.

Jess mouth was hesitant against hers. Kissing carefully against the cut in Sam's bottom lip.

Sam chuckled. "No need to be a lamb, baby. Take what you need."

The cab was silent save for the hitch of Jess' breathing. Soft fingers danced over Sam's cheek and across her bottom lip. Jess' hungry eyes held Sam's, the flames of her anger still smoldering in the depths. Sam had seen this look more times than she could count. Remembered being trapped in that gaze. Prey frozen in the presence of a predator. Sam never minded being hunted by Jess. She loved it. Craved it. And never once had she been scared by it.

Jess' lips crashed onto hers. Skin split and spilled blood—hot and metallic—into their mouths. Buttons popped and bounced to the floor of the cab. Nails dug into skin, tearing at the fabric covering Sam's chest until it clung to her shoulders by thin strips of white cloth. Teeth scraped across her skin and Sam groaned.

"That's it, baby," Sam sighed.

Bloody kisses marred her skin. Trailed down her neck and dotted her collarbone. A red ring encircled Sam's nipple, Jess latched to the other one while she clawed at the button of Sam's shorts until Sam helped her.

The cab shuddered and rocked as Jess shoved her underwear to the side and took all of Sam in a single thrust. Sam choked out a cry. She had missed this. The raw vulnerability of it all. Of baring the ugliness living in both of them and embracing it. Sam had loved watching Jess fight for her as much as Jess reveled in making them fear her. And she loved each burst of pain from Jess' teeth marking her skin. A feral declaration of ownership.

This is mine and no one else can have it.

Chapter 10

JESS TRIED NOT TO stare at the way Sam held her shirt closed as they walked up the gravel driveway with their hands entwined. Dried blood crusted her bottom lip and where Jess had smeared it over her chin. The bruise on her cheek bloomed and red marks dotted her neck and dipped down, hidden by the shirt pulled taut across Sam's chest.

For the first time that night, Jess' hands were throbbing, feeling every bit as raw as they looked. James' teeth had flayed her knuckles open. Brown blood dried stiff against her skin. Her scalp ached from where Sam had twisted Jess' hair in her hands, but that was a welcome pain.

"Want to bet Ma already knows what happened?" Sam said, trying to inject cheer into her voice as they stepped onto the porch together.

"Maybe not the truth but I'm sure Sheriff called your father and then he called your mother." Jess hesitated. "D'you think she'll turn me in and get mad at Lily for lying?"

"Considering she hates that Lily is dating that asshole, *and* he started this mess, no, I don't think so." Sam pressed a soft kiss to her knuckles. "Let's go in and get cleaned up. I'm ready to relax and forget about what happened."

"I don't want to forget everything," Jess mumbled.

Sam grinned.

Juniper paced in the kitchen, the cordless tucked in between her ear and her shoulder and the other hand waving her book around as she spoke in a loud whisper. As soon as the screen door opened, she stopped, relief clouding her panicked expression.

"They just walked in," she said to whoever was on the other end, probably Keith. "Yeah, I'll be heading home in a bit. Just get Lily home."

The cordless slammed into the charger with a click. Juniper whirled to face them properly, eyes darting over the bruises on Sam's cheek and the state of Jess' hands.

"That was your father. He went to the Sheriff's to pick up Lily. Seems some out-of-towners jumped James and he's had to go to the hospital."

Neither Jess nor Sam said anything.

"What really happened?" Juniper pressed. "And no bullshit. I'll damn well know if you're lying."

"Some assholes started bothering us. James came over and started trouble, telling them..." Sam drifted off a moment and cleared her throat. "Told them who I was, and they didn't take it well."

"They followed us to the truck," Jess added. "Started hitting Sam."

"And what did you do?" Juniper asked Jess.

"There was a wrench in the truck."

"Did you hit James with the wrench too?"

Jess shook her head. "They ran. He didn't. I hit him too."

Juniper's eyes strayed down. "Seems like you did more than that. Where is the wrench?"

"In the truck," Sam answered.

"Well, at least you didn't leave it behind." Juniper scrubbed her hand down her face. "James is in the hospital. Broken nose. Swelling. Not sure if anything else right now."

Jess swallowed.

Juniper narrowed her eyes. "When someone brings it up you better act really damn surprised. You went to the fair and had a very nice time, but you didn't see shit. Do you understand?"

"Yes ma'am," they both mumbled.

Juniper grabbed her book and tucked it into her purse on the table. "I'm going to meet Keith at home and talk to Lily. Since she's already decided to lie for you, I'm going to make sure she doesn't slip up and get in trouble for it."

"Thanks, Ma," Sam whispered, hanging her head.

Juniper sighed. "I'm not angry at you Sam. You don't deserve this kind of shit, and frankly, I'm glad someone taught that little shit a lesson. But I do wish it had been someone else instead of you two."

"Sorry," Jess said.

Juniper patted her arm. "Now, you'll need to be buying yourself a new wrench. You don't have one anymore. In fact, you lost it a long time ago. Bring the truck home tomorrow for a good cleaning." She carefully kissed Sam's cheek.

"Is your momma really going to destroy evidence," Jess said as Juniper rushed from the house to her car parked by the ditch.

"If I didn't know any better, I'd say she has experience." Sam shook her head and closed the front door. "That went better than I thought."

"Shower?" Jess asked.

Sam nodded.

"You go ahead first. I'm going to check on Momma real quick."

Sam kissed Jess' temple and disappeared upstairs. The pipes groaned as the shower turned on. Jess walked through the downstairs, turning off lights in the kitchen—pausing to grab the baby monitor from the table—and living room before walking down the hallway. She stood in the doorway, watching the small huddled mass under the sheets. When she couldn't see the rise and fall of her mother's chest, she tiptoed closer.

Aveline's gnarled fingers grasped the sheets under her neck. Air whistled out of her nose as she breathed in and out. Shadows danced under her eyes. Jess gently reached and pushed away a wisp of gray tickling her mother's cheek.

"Lottie?" Momma muttered, eyes barely opening. "Is that you, again? I told you I didn't like you coming in here while I'm sleeping."

"No, Momma, it's just me," Jess whispered. "I was just checking in on you."

"Oh, Jessamine." Aveline smacked her lips together. "Tell Lottie to stay out of my room. She scares me."

"Who is Lottie?"

Aveline didn't answer. Breath ghosted over parted lips. Her chest rose and fell. Believing her momma had fallen back asleep, Jess turned back to the doorway.

"Go away, Lottie!"

Jess jumped, whirling around to where Momma sat up in bed, eyes wide with terror, and clutching the sheet to her chest with trembling fingers.

"It's just me, Momma, no one else is here," Jess hissed, heart thundering in her chest. "Why are you yelling?"

"You can't fool me," Aveline's voice shook. "I know why you've come, and you can't. You can't have her. Neither of you can."

Jess took a step forward and Aveline wailed. The overhead light clicked on, momentarily blinding Jess. Spots danced in her vision, and she blinked, trying to rid herself of them.

"I heard yelling, is everything okay?" Sam said from the doorway, panting as she held a towel around herself, blond hair plastered to her skin.

Aveline held a hand in front of her eyes and squinted at them. "Oh, Jessamine, Sam." She smoothed her hair down. "Why are you in my room? And what on earth happened to your face, Sam?"

Sam touched her cheek and grimaced. "Just a bit of a tussle, Miss Aveline. Nothing to worry about. Are you alright?"

"Oh, I'm quite alright. Just had an odd dream...I think." Aveline's brow furrowed. "I think I'd like to get back to sleep now."

"Are you sure you're okay, Momma? You were saying weird things," Jess said. "You were talking about Lottie again."

"I don't know anyone named Lottie," Aveline snapped. "Now if you don't mind, it's late and I don't want to be gawked at in my sleep by my daughter and her lover. So, if you don't mind."

Sam's hand curled around Jess' elbow. "Come on, let's let your momma sleep."

Jess turned off the light as she left the room, her heart still beating erratically. "She's lying."

Sam hummed in agreement. "But what can you do if she's not willing to tell you."

Tension made Jess' back ache. For once, she'd like a straight answer from her mother. About anything.

"You know, Misty gave me something as a welcome home gift and I'd been saving it. Tonight seems like a good night, considering the shit that happened," Jess huffed, rubbing her temples. "Care to split a joint?"

Sam chuckled. "Now you tell me you have weed in the house."

"Have you stopped smoking? Do I need to get rid of it?"

"Nothing like that. But I…sort of brought some with me in case you were interested." Sam leaned against the banister. "Why don't you shower, and I'll meet you in your room with some snacks. We'll clean up your hands first, okay?"

Jess nodded, soft smile tugging at her lips as Sam kissed her forehead. "I won't be long."

Water stung the open wounds. She hissed as she carefully washed away the crusted blood from the raw edges until all she saw was pink and red skin. Clear fluid oozed from cuts.

She quickly washed the rest of her aching body, the warm spray draining the tension from her body until all she felt was a bone-deep exhaustion. Episodes like that always took everything out of her. All these years away she had kept her temper reined in as often as she could. Sometimes to her own detriment. Jess either simmered, constantly stewing in anger, or exploded and lost all control. Sam had been the only one able to get her back, and that was still true.

Does it hurt her when I'm like this?

Jess pressed the heels of her hands to her eyes. What if she took Sam down with her one of these days? Jess wouldn't be able to live with herself. Wouldn't be able to look at herself in the mirror anymore.

"Feel better?" Sam asked as Jess crossed the threshold into their room.

"A bit."

Sam reclined against Jess' headboard, her legs stretched out in front of her, and the baggie with two joints already sitting on the nightstand next to a can of chips and bottles of water. The old metal first aid kit sat in her lap.

"Care to join me?" Sam held her hand out.

Jess took her hand and climbed onto the bed next to Sam, clutching to towel to her chest to keep it from falling open. Not that Sam would mind. Sam carefully swabbed antibiotic ointment over the cuts before bandaging each one until all of Jess' fingers were adorned with a flesh-colored bandage—not the color of her flesh, but of someone's, the tan a stark contrast to her pale pink fingers.

"How bad does it hurt?" Sam asked.

"I could ask you the same thing."

Sam shrugged. "Not the first time I've been punched. Won't be the last."

"It will be if I have anything to say about it."

Sam smirked. "There you go. Ready to fight the world for me." She kissed the bandaged knuckles. "You can't take on everyone."

"Says you," Jess muttered.

Sam brushed damp strands behind Jess' ear. "There are other ways of triumphing against most hateful assholes."

"Like what?"

"Like living." Sam kissed the inside of Jess' wrist. "Loving." Her mouth moved up Jess' forearm. "Being who I am out of sheer spite, and finding my happiness where I can."

"With me?" Jess' voice trembled, afraid that Sam would say no. Afraid she would say yes.

Was Jess really worth loving?

"Yes," Sam breathed, cupping Jess' cheek. "I meant what I said Jess. I love you. I never stopped. If you don't feel the same, then I can accept that, but my heart belongs to you either way."

"What if I've done things?" Jess whispered.

"I can't imagine anything you've done that would change my mind."

Jess pursed her quivering lips.

Sam' thumb brushed her cheek. "Tell me, sweetheart. Tell me what you saw."

"What do you mean?" Jess' brow furrowed in confusion.

"When you were hitting James, you weren't just hitting him, were you?"

Jess looked away.

"You can tell me, Jess, I promise," Sam murmured. "If you want to tell me, I'm right here."

Jess' eyes flicked to the joints. "You might want to light one. I'm going to get comfortable."

Sam nodded. "Okay."

The pungent smell of weed filled the small room. Jess pulled on soft sleep shorts covered in small pink sheep and a matching pink tank top. Eyes bored into her back as she cracked open the window to let out the smell and let in the almost cool breeze, fall trying to push summer out.

Springs creaked under Jess' knees as she climbed over Sam and tucked herself against the wall. Sam handed over the joint, blowing a cloud of smoke into the air, and waited.

"His name was Garth," Jess mumbled, fitting the joint between her lips and dragging in a lungful of smoke. "We met when I was bartending. He'd come in with his friends and always tip me extra for taking good care of them. Flirted all the damn time, but I didn't think much of it then."

"When did you start dating?" Sam took the joint back.

Jess leaned her head against the wall. "Not for months. He scribbled his number on a napkin, but I never called him. Was too worried I'd get fired for it because we had just switched managers, and the new one was a hardass. Then one night, he saw me on a night off. I was at a club with some...acquaintances, and he bought me a few drinks and we got to talking.

He was from a small town too. Knew how jarring the city was but also how freeing. Though, we both agreed that sometimes it was too fucking loud. He gave me his number again and since it wasn't at work, I was like fuck it. We started casually dating and after a few months it got serious."

"What happened when it got serious?"

"He came with me when I moved to start at uni; he was a day laborer, so it wasn't too hard for him to find work. We shared that little off-campus apartment. Things were perfect for a while. I thought…" she trailed off and took a hit, her mind finally going hazy at the edges. "I thought everything was perfect. That he was it for me. Marriage. Kids. A cute little house instead of an apartment."

Sam squeezed Jess' knee and waited.

"You know, I always used to wonder why women didn't just pick up and leave. I thought they were weak for staying with someone who could hurt them. Wondered why they would be with an abuser at all." Jess shook her head. "And then that woman was me. I had fallen in love with someone who was charming and funny and sweet so when he smacked me that first time, I thought it had to be my fault. That I had to have done something awful to push someone normally so kind into violence."

Sam was frozen against the headboard, joint clenched in her fingers.

Jess swallowed. "I told him so much about myself and he used all of it against me. Told me I was fucked up, but it was okay because he loved me anyway. Would goad me into arguments and then fuck me until I bled, because 'violence excites you' and 'every couple has make-up sex after a fight' even though I didn't want it."

"Fuck," Sam swore softly.

Jess' nose burned. She closed her eyes to hold hot tears at bay. "When he found the positive pregnancy test in the trash can, he punched me so hard I blacked out. I came to and he was screaming at me to get rid of it and then he left. Didn't tell me where was going.

Didn't come back for two days." She ran shaky hands through her hair. "When he came back, he was sweet and told me he was sorry. Told me that he was just scared at first, but now he was happy that we could start a family. But I didn't want to anymore. Not with him."

"Did you...?" Sam trailed off, gently handing the joint back over.

"I miscarried." Jess' sob turned into a sharp laugh. "I never thought I'd be happy for something like that to happen. But I was also, sad and...it hurt more than I thought it would for something I decided I didn't want. He didn't even care. Didn't even look up from the game when I told him I was bleeding. I had to call a cab to take me to the emergency room. Alone."

"I'm so sorry, Jess," Sam's anguished voice was hushed. "I wish I had been there for you. I—"

Jess slowly laid down, stretching out beside Sam, and lying her head on Sam's thigh. "You were there in a way. When I was sitting in that room alone, I thought of you. Pretended that you were holding my hand, not the nurse, when the doctor confirmed I miscarried. And when I went back to the apartment, you were there with me, telling me it was time to leave."

"Did you leave then?"

"No," Jess whispered. "I tried, but he'd get angrier and angrier every time I tried so I just...stopped. I stopped fighting. Stopped yelling back. When he'd do things or say things, I wouldn't react at all." She huffed a soft laugh. "He got bored of me, I think. What was the fun if I wouldn't fight back so he could exert himself over me."

"Jess—"

"He found someone else. Someone cute and bubbly and he'd always be gone." She shook her head. "Something...snapped, I think. I was angry that he could just break me and walk away. Scared that he'd do to her what he did to me. I was so furious and then, there was just a blank moment. I don't know how or why, but I was in the apartment and then I was standing outside hers, holding a knife and banging on the door while the cops were yelling at me to drop the knife."

"Fuck," Sam repeated, brushing her fingers through Jess' hair.

"I was arrested. He told them I was just some crazy ex-girlfriend. I told them everything."

"Did they arrest him?"

Jess shook her head. "No evidence. No reports. I called Celia because I didn't know who else to call. Big fucking mistake on my part."

"She didn't help?"

"She had me committed."

Sam craned her neck to look down at Jess. "She what?"

"Apparently, the lawyer advised her that due to my circumstances and my confession, I might be able to get out of going to jail if I agreed to an 'in-patient program' which I wouldn't have. Celia made the choice for me. Checked me in against my will and when those hours were up, the judge had already agreed to my in-patient treatment." Jess picked at a white sheep on her shorts. "She called me once to tell me what was happening, and then didn't call me again until she was coming to get me to bring me here."

Sam leaned back. "That's cold even for her."

"Tell me about it."

Sam brushed her fingers over Jess' cheek. "I should've found a way to go with you that night. If we had stayed together maybe..."

Jess turned her head and kissed Sam's fingers. "Maybe this still would've happened anyway. Maybe you wouldn't have learned about yourself if you had stayed with me. Lord knows, I was a wreck waiting to happen."

"I don't believe that."

"Well, you've always given me more credit than I thought I deserved."

Sam placed what was left of the joint in a small glass ashtray on the nightstand. She slid down the headboard until she lay flush with Jess, their foreheads touching. "I think you're incredible."

"Even now?"

"I told you my feelings wouldn't change, and they haven't. All I wish is that I could've swooped in and saved you when you needed me."

Jess traced the curve of Sam's jaw. "I need you now," she whispered in the dwindling space between them.

"You have me."

A soft shuffling woke Sam. She sat up in Celia's old bed—though she distinctly remembered falling asleep in Jess' bed—and blinked in the hazy moonlit room. Jess' bed was empty. Sheets lay in a heap on the floor and the bedroom door was wide open. The plastic baby monitor sat on the nightstand, light flickering green with only the gentle static of Aveline's breathing coming through.

Sam cursed.

Her footsteps padded across the warm wooden floor as she hurried into the hallway, unsure of where Jess might have walked off to, and hoping she wasn't underneath the house again. Seeing Jess walk into the kitchen, trembling and covered in mud, had scared Sam enough. She didn't want it to happen again.

The door to Jess' grandfather's room was cracked. Warmth bled away the closer Sam stepped to the room. Cold air seeped from the opening and Sam shivered. She placed her hand on the knob to open the door and froze.

Jess lay on the bed, arms and legs splayed and her head turned to the side. But that wasn't what made Sam's blood turn into an icy sludge of fear.

A shadow loomed over the bed. Long fingers—or tendrils, Sam wasn't sure—brushed over Jess' face and down her neck. Dark shapes wriggled over her body like fat little garden worms. The shadow leaned down as if to kiss Jess.

No!

Sam pushed open the door and darted in, prepared to fight whatever spectral intruder was trying to harm Jess, but the room was empty. Still freezing cold, but empty. Jess was curled up on her side, her back to the door. Breath rattled in Sam's lungs. She hadn't imagined the shadow.

Had she?

They had smoked both joints before finally falling asleep. Perhaps the haziness had lingered, meshing dreams with reality. Sam brushed her hand down her face. That had to be it. Just an odd waking dream. The shadow of things Jess had shared mixing with the fear Sam had when she woke and found Jess gone.

"Jess," she murmured, gently shaking Jess' shoulder. "Baby, come back to bed."

Jess mumbled something unintelligible.

"What was that?"

"Don't be mad at me Momma, Pawpaw told me I could sleep here," Jess grumbled.

"Nobody is mad, Jess," Sam promised. "You're dreaming, sweetheart. You walked in here."

"I didn't walk. Pawpaw carried me," Jess whined. "Let me sleep; I'm so tired."

Sam sighed and kissed Jess' shoulder. "I would feel better if you were in your own bed." She didn't want Jess in this room, shadow or no shadow. "It'll just be a minute and then you can go right back to sleep, okay?"

Jess whined and huffed as if she were a child again but rolled over and stood up from the bed. She leaned heavily on Sam as they walked back to her room.

"Don't you hear that?" Jess whispered.

"Hear what?"

"The baby," Jess mumbled. "It won't stop crying. It's making him mad."

"What are you—?"

Jess gasped and doubled over, clutching her stomach with one hand while the other wrapped around the banister. A shaky sob fell from her lips.

"What's wrong? What hurts?"

Jess curled into herself as much as possible. Sam's eyes searched for any visible problems. Maybe something she had missed during the earlier fight. Had Jess been hurt and she hadn't noticed? Her eyes landed on the red staining the crotch of Jess' sleep shorts. Beads of blood dripped thin red rivers down her thigh.

Oh.

This she could handle.

She walked Jess to the bathroom and helped her sit in the tub. Jess blinked blearily in the bright lights. Sleep still had hold of her. She rubbed her eyes and winced, clutching her side.

"Can you tell me where you keep the pads, Jess?" Sam asked, opening the mirror cabinet but only found a razor and bottle of ibuprofen. She hesitated giving Jess anything right now, unsure of how it might interact with the weed. She didn't want to take any chances.

"Hall closet," Jess finally mumbled.

The door to Jess' grandfather's room remained open. Yawning darkness blacking out what the moonlight had lit before. Everything about that room made Sam uneasy. She felt as if she were being watched. Toyed with. Mocked. She stomped across the hall and pulled the door shut. That didn't make her feel much better.

She pushed the feelings out of her mind to tend for Jess. Helping her clean up and getting her back into bed was far more important. Sam slept out on the outside, keeping Jess trapped against the wall. If she wanted to walk again, she would have to climb over Sam first, and Sam would wake in time to stop her. Sam pressed against Jess' back and kissed her temple.

"Sorry," Jess mumbled.

"It's okay." Sam rubbed her arm. "Just get some sleep. I'm right here."

Jess sighed. Seconds ticking by. "Love you," she whispered before her breath evened out.

Chapter 11

SUMMER REFUSED TO LEAVE. Humidity clung to Jess' skin. Smothered her lungs with damp every time she drew breath. Bugs screamed in the grass and the trees, yelling their disdain for the heat that covered the county like a hot, wet blanket. Jess stood at the sink, fanning herself with a paper plate while staring out the window at the pond.

Her knee itched.

Jess absently scratched at the cut on her knee. Nearly a month since she scraped herself up by falling in the pond and it hadn't gone away. She rinsed bright red blood from her fingers under the tap and wet a cloth to dab at the reopened wound.

The screen door creaked open, and Jess turned to watch Lily walk inside with a paper bag stamped with the name of the general store up the road. She and Lily hadn't spoken since that night. Jess didn't know if Lily was angry or scared or a muddied mix of both. Neither said anything as Lily pulled out the kitchen chair and plopped down, tossing the bag onto the table.

"This heat is bullshit," she grumbled, wiping the set from her forehead. "Got any tea?"

Jess tossed the bloodied cloth into the sink and reached into the closest cupboard for two glasses. A nice cold glass of iced tea might do her some good. Hopefully cool down the warmth bubbling under her skin.

"Thanks," Lily said, taking a swig and setting the glass back down. She didn't look at Jess. Not yet. Instead, her eyes strayed to the brown spots crawling along the floor underneath the pantry, freckling the bottom half of the door. "Fuck, is that mold?"

Jess shook her head. "Sam had tested some and sent it off, but nope. Not mold. No fucking clue what it is."

"Huh." Lily pushed the bag closer. "Sam asked me to pick these things up for you while she's at work. Said you're having the period from hell."

Jess tilted the bag and looked inside. Two packs of orange pads were nestled amongst a pack of chocolate chip cookies and a bottle of ibuprofen. "Almost two weeks," she grumbled, leaning back until the chair creaked. "I feel like shit."

"Sorry."

Jess shrugged.

"I also wanted to tell you that the sheriff's couldn't find the assholes who jumped James. The case is open but also sort of closed. No one's interested in looking and the chances of finding those guys are pretty slim." Lily took another nonchalant sip of her tea.

"Why did you lie for me?"

"You're family."

"And he was your boyfriend."

Lily looked away. "You know, the entire time we dated he told me he didn't have a problem with Sam. That he didn't agree with his parents or anyone else. He never said anything bad to me, but I believed him. Then he was drinking at the fair and he saw you two together, and I finally saw it." She sighed and gathered her blond hair away from her neck. "The disgust on his face. I hadn't seen it before. I tried to keep him away. Figured I could dump him when he wasn't drunk, and then…everything else just happened."

"I'm sorry he lied to you," Jess muttered.

"Yeah, well, I'm sorry that I didn't do more."

"Then he would've hit you."

"You think?"

"Eventually."

They drank their tea in silence. In the room over, Aveline gently snored in her chair, exhausted from the oppressive heat.

Lily drained her glass and stood to take it to the sink. "Do you need anything else?"

"No, but thanks. I'll be fine until Sam gets home."

"Good. Momma didn't say I was out and out grounded, but she's encouraged me to keep my head down for now."

"For the best," Jess agreed. "At least, until this blows over."

Lily nodded. "Listen, Jess. If James tells his father—"

"I'll handle the Reverend if he comes around, and I won't let him touch your sister," Jess promised. "You don't have to worry."

"I believe you. I just…it's been nice to see Sam this happy. I hope you'll stick around."

Jess gestured around with a smirk. "Where else would I go?"

Lily snorted. "See you around then. Hope you feel better."

The screen door closed. A gentle breeze finally wafted through the open windows and Jess sighed, the sheen of sweat on her skin cooling for a brief moment. She should move to the couch. Try to glean as much cold air from Momma's window AC as she could and rest until Sam returned. That's all she did lately. Sleep. Sometimes walking, sometimes dreaming. Either way Sam tried her best to settle Jess back into bed nearly every single night. Their routine took a toll on them both.

It's all my fault.

Maybe she should try the pills again. Sure, they made her feel foggy and sluggish, barely able to string together a coherent thought, but maybe then she could sleep and stay asleep.

Pain like a knife dug into her back and radiated in waves down to her knees. Jess winced, reaching into the paper bag on the table for the ibuprofen.

Two weeks of awful cramps, headaches, and heavy bleeding sapped all of her energy. When she wasn't taking medicine to combat the cramps that seized up her legs and her back with a constant ache, she was blowing through pads like tissue. She could barely get out of the shower without blood tricking down her leg or worse, a thick, dark mass plopping onto the floor and splattering blood and ichor over her ankles and feet.

She washed down the ibuprofen with the last of her iced tea and curled inward, resting her cheek on her folded arms. Heavy heat cloaked her like a blanket and tugged her eyelids closed. The loud cacophony of screaming bugs turned into a melody, luring her further into the darkness that waited with open arms.

"Jessamine," a low voice growled in her ear.

Heat seared her knee and her eyes flew open. Her soft cry ghosted across her arm. Wet dripped down her leg. Droplets growing bigger and bigger until they poured down her leg in a sheet. Jess tried to sit up. Tried to look. She couldn't move. Something hard—like a bony finger—pressed against the wound. Poking and tugging at the raw edges of flesh.

Tears clung to her vision. She opened her mouth to cry, scream, something that would get Aveline's attention from where she slumbered in her recliner. No sounds came out.

The finger pressed into the wound, flaying it open with a wet squelch. Jess heaved at the shockwaves of pain radiating into the bone and up her thighs, and the wriggling sensation thrusting and undulating under her skin.

"Jessamine!"

Jess shot up from the kitchen table, breaths squeezing out of her lungs and tears cascading down her cheeks. She pushed the chair back from the table and readied herself for the gaping hole in her skin. The knee was inflamed from where she had scratched it earlier, but otherwise unchanged.

"My gosh, darlin'," Derotha said, watching Jess with concern wrinkling the space between her brows. "You must've been having some dream."

Jess leaned her elbows on the table and hid her face, fingers hastily brushing tears. "Sorry, Miss Derotha. Must've been the ibuprofen."

"Not feeling well still?"

Jess shook her head.

"Well, your momma is my last appointment for the day. I can stay a little longer until Sam gets home if you want to go rest."

Normally, Jess would turn her down. It was too much to ask. Derotha worked so hard for all of her patients already. Jess didn't want to take away any time for herself. But Jess' sanity was clinging on by a thread. She needed sleep. At least a few hours of uninterrupted sleep. No dreaming. No walking.

Jess nodded. "Thank you. I just need a little bit of rest."

"Go on." Derotha waved her away. "I have things handled for now. Don't you fret about nothing and just get some sleep, poor dear."

Jess offered a watery smile and leaned on the table to stand. Despite the pain being a dream, her legs still shook, and she clung to the banister while pulling herself up the stairs. The heat was even worse upstairs even with her bedroom window open. She thought about opening Pawpaw's window for a cross breeze but every time she went to open the door, her stomach roiled in protest.

Flopping down onto the top sheet, she curled onto her side and tucked her pillow under her neck. Jess closed her eyes and desperately willed sleep to come. Minutes ticked by. She was painfully aware of the stillness of the air, a breeze refusing to bless her with a cool kiss, and the shuffling sounds coming from downstairs as Derotha moved around. Sleep lingered on the edge. Playing a game of keep away like a child. Jess would get close, and sleep would run in the other direction.

Drip, drip, drip.

A sob burst past her chapped lips. She turned her face into her pillow, whispering pleas to a god who hadn't listened in a long time, but she hoped beyond hope that his ear was turned to her now.

Drip, drip, drip.

The sound came from the bathroom, but she refused to get up. It felt like a trap. Another dream waiting to worm its way into unconsciousness. Torment her until she gave up on sleep completely and succumbed to losing her mind. Her knee began to ache. She clenched her jaw and shoved her face further into the pillow.

Maybe if she smothered herself this would end?

Pain flared in her knee and she shot up with a gasp. She risked a look. Thin black lines spread from the cut, pulsating as blood pumped through her veins. Jess gasped. She poked at the cut. Black ichor oozed from the wound.

Her stomach rolled. Bile rose in her throat. Wobbly legs carried her to the bathroom where she collapsed in front of the toilet. The porcelain clanged as she pushed open the lid and braced.

Jess dry-heaved. Over and over again. Nothing came up. Her throat ached. More tears welled in the corners of her eyes. She couldn't sleep. Couldn't vomit. Nothing of her body listened to her.

"Please," she begged to the unmoving water in the bowl, her stomach clenching in agony. "Just get it over with."

Drip, drip, drip.

Soft fingers dragged through her hair, pulling strands away from her face. She hadn't heard Sam come in. Had she laid in bed that long or had Sam come home early to take care of her? Jess leaned into the touch, eyes fluttering closed, and sighed in relief.

"I'm glad you're here," she mumbled.

Wet pressed against her back, seeping into her shirt. Her brow furrowed. Had Sam taken a dip in the pond or something? She knew it was hot, but Sam would at least change into a swimsuit first.

Her gut clenched and Jess doubled over once more, shaking over the bowl. Still nothing came.

"Poor thing," a scratchy voice that did not belong to her girlfriend, whispered in her ear. "Let me help."

Jess gasped and two fingers forced their way into her mouth. She tried to move her head but a firm hand held her chin in an iron grip. She scratched at the arms holding her still. Skin tore away. Wedged under her fingernails. Blood and pus stained her fingertips. Chunks came away and plopped onto the floor with wet splats. Her teeth sank into loamy flesh that burst like a tomato. Thick pus filled her mouth, the putrid taste of infection lingering on her tongue, and she gagged.

A third finger slunk into her mouth. Forced her lips open wide. Pus sluiced down her throat, constricting as it moved the thick sludge down into her stomach. The hand tilted her face down over the toilet as everything she ate that day sprayed from her mouth. Flecks of partially digested eggs and toast splattered the sides of the toilet. She heaved over and over. Acid burned its way up her throat and rushed around the fingers.

There was nothing left in her stomach, but she couldn't stop. Liquid, a murky brown that reminded her of the water in the pond, gushed from her open lips. The water in the toilet turned the same brackish color. Rose higher and higher as the fingers forced their way further, touching the back of her tongue. Water spilled over, splashing onto her and spreading across the floor.

Her eyes rolled back. Her lungs screamed for air. Black spots danced in her vision.

The water kept coming. Kept spilling from her mouth. Silt dried on her cheeks. Jess collapsed into the body holding her up. The hand tilted her chin up. She would've screamed if she could. Flesh hung from bone. Teeth flashed through holes in skin. Water dripped from the black hole where a nose had been. She stared into dark, pocked, sockets where eyes should've been.

The hand gently stroked her neck and down her torso. It pressed against her swelling belly. Teeth flashed in what she thought looked much like a smile.

"You were always my favorite," the words crawled up from its throat, but it's mouth didn't move.

Her sob turned into a desperate gurgle.

"My dear Jessamine. Welcome home."

The silver bell wound around the handle jingled as Sam pushed open the door for the diner. Booths and tables sat empty, waiting for the dinner rush to come through like a tornado. Sam was thankful. She wasn't much in the mood for being stared at while she ordered food to take home to Jess.

"Hey, hun," Darlene greeted from the other side of the counter, pink pen tucked behind her ear. "Jess still not feeling well?"

Sam sighed and ran her fingers through her hair and slid onto a stool. "Not really. Is it...normal to last this long?"

Darlene popped her gum and nodded. "Sometimes. Could be changes, stress, something else going on. Might be time to take her up to the doctor and see what they say."

"She hates doctors."

"We all hate doctors," Darlene chuckled. "They never warm their hands, and they always want to have small talk when they're rootin' around between our legs."

Sam choked on a laugh.

"There's a laugh." Darlene smiled. "Want me to pack up the usual?"

"Please," Sam answered, still laughing under her breath. "I'm hoping it'll help Jess feel better."

"Well, I'm sure an extra slice of cake will do the trick." Darlene winked.

"Thanks."

Sam drummed her fingers on the counter in time to The Beach Boys song playing on the jukebox. The grill sizzled in the kitchen and Darlene hummed in the back. Sam stared at the pictures behind the counter. Old black and white photos from years past. There were even pictures of her parents somewhere on the wall. A picture right above the coffee pots caught her eye.

"Hey, Darlene," she called.

"Hmm?" Darlene poked her head around the corner. "Forget something?"

"Oh no, I was just wondering about one of the pictures." Sam pointed to the one in question. "I was wondering if I could get a closer look."

Darlene's heels clicked against the floor as she grabbed the picture from the wall and set it on the counter. "I didn't even realize we had this one."

Four teenagers sat in the corner booth of the diner. Sam immediately recognized the youthful face of her father, beardless and without the lines in his face from years of heavy work and wide smiles. Across from him sat a young Reverend Daniels, not yet the collared asshole Sam despised, holding hands with Aveline. Sam didn't know they had dated as teenagers. Then again, none of them really spoke about those years, not even her own father.

Tucked in-between Aveline and Keith sat a young woman that Sam would've sworn was Jess. Her hair was longer and pulled back in a thick headband, but the crinkle of her eyes and wide smile were nearly identical.

"Who is this woman?" Sam asked, tapping her finger on the glass.

Darlene leaned over and pressed her lips together. "That would be Lottie. Goodness, I haven't thought about her in years."

"Who is Lottie?"

Darlene straightened and sighed. "I'm surprised no one told you. She's Aveline's sister."

"I didn't know Miss Aveline ever had a sister. Jess had never mentioned an aunt."

Darlene nodded solemnly. "I'm not surprised at that. Aveline was heartbroken when Lottie up and left town one day. She never really spoke of her again. Probably too angry that Lottie had left Aveline alone with their father."

"Why was that bad thing?"

"I'm not sure I should say much more," Darlene murmured. "I don't know what kind of memories Jess has of her grandfather, but when I was growing up, he was a mean sonofabitch. Put his daughters through hell and back. Lottie...well, I reckon when she found out she was pregnant, she up and ran to keep her kids away from him. I don't blame her one bit."

"She ran?"

"Disappeared one night and no one ever saw her again. Your poor father was heartbroken." She leaned close and whispered as if there were anyone in the dining room but them: "He was sweet on her all those years ago. Pretty sure he planned on marrying her even though, rumor has it, the baby wasn't his."

Sam leaned away. "Really? He never talked about her at all."

"Yeah, I can imagine it was too painful for him. Not knowing what happened to her all these years." Darlene sighed and picked up the picture to hang it back up. "I felt bad for those girls growing up living with a man like that. I couldn't fathom why Aveline stayed and had two little girls in that house with him, but I suppose things worked out how they're meant to."

A bell dinged in the kitchen.

"Let me go pack up your food real quick, hun." Darlene disappeared in the back once more.

Lottie being Aveline's sister made sense. They were in pictures wearing matching dresses. Why was Lottie's soiled dress from her childhood tucked away in a box? Had it been tucked away and forgotten or had it been kept for a purpose? Sam returned to drumming on the counter. Did any of it really matter or was Sam trying to think of something to take her mind off of what was happening to Jess?

Something was clearly wrong. She wasn't well. Physically. Mentally. But Sam didn't know how to help and what kind of help Jess would be open to receiving. If Sam suggested a therapist, Jess might balk and think Sam was trying to lock her away in a hospital like Celia did. Feeling abandoned wouldn't help Jess. Would she let Sam take her to a regular doctor? Maybe they could frame things in a way that Jess would accept.

No, she's too fucking stubborn.

Sam huffed and dragged her fingers through her hair and checked her watch. The hand was ticking closer to five. She wanted to get home before people flooded the diner.

Darlene rounded the corner with two bags and set them on the counter. "You make sure to tell Jess I hope she feels better."

Sam reached into her pocket and pulled out her wallet. She slid the cash across the counter—with a tip for Darlene—and grasped the handles of the paper bags. "Thanks, Darlene, I will."

"Have a good one, Sam."

Sam walked out and stopped short, almost crashing into the Reverend.

"Oh, Sam." Reverend Daniels blinked, dark circles carved under his eyes. "I didn't see you."

Sam swallowed her snarky retort. "It's alright, Reverend. Going in?"

"I...yes," he answered. "I apologize. I've been so tired lately."

"I heard about James. I hope he's recovering," Sam said.

She didn't entirely mean it. Frankly, her thoughts hadn't strayed to James at all considering how much of her focus stayed on Jess. And as far as she was concerned, James had riled up those men to do the same thing. They probably would have succeeded in killing Sam, not to mention what they would've done to Jess.

"Thank you," he whispered. "That's kind of you."

Kinder than you fucking deserve.

Sam's smile was tight. "Have a good night."

The ride home was quiet. She didn't even bother turning on the radio as she pulled on the dirt road and bounced all the way to the house, pulling in behind Aveline's still broken-down car. Parts were on back order and Sam hadn't worried too much about it lately.

Derotha looked up from the couch as Sam walked into the house and let the screen door close behind her. Aveline sat in her recliner, as usual, but Jess was nowhere to be found.

Panic seized Sam's heart.

"Poor thing looked like a wrung out dishrag," Derotha said before Sam could ask. "I offered to stay a little extra time and visit with Aveline so Jess could rest until you got home."

Sam's shoulders dropped. "Thank you. Has she been sleeping this whole time?"

"Haven't heard a peep so I sure hope so." Derotha stood.

"Thank you, really, Derotha, I—"

Derotha patted Sam's arm and smiled. "Don't worry too much. Some decent rest and she'll be right as rain."

Sam wasn't sure, but she nodded. "Have a good night, Miss Derotha."

Derotha waved to Aveline before breezing out the door with her bag slung over her shoulder. The house settled into an uneasy quiet. Aveline kept watching the TV with vacant eyes, light dancing across her wrinkled face. Nothing came from upstairs. No footsteps or crying. Sam left the bags on the kitchen table and carefully ascended, eyes searching for evidence that Jess hadn't been resting.

The door to her grandfather's room was shut tight. Sam breathed in relief. The door to the bathroom sat open as did the door to the room they shared. Sam poked her head inside and saw Jess lying on her side, facing the wall, the sheet and the blanket pulled tight to her chin. It was far too hot for all those covers.

Sam frowned.

The bed dipped as she sat on the edge. "Jess," she murmured, carefully brushing damp strands of hair away from Jess' face. "Baby?"

Jess mumbled and pulled the blanket tighter.

Sam pressed the back of her hand to Jess' forehead. "Shit."

Heat blazed against her hand. Droplets of sweat clung to her skin. She wiped her hand on her jumpsuit. How long had Jess been like this?

"Baby, can you talk to me?" Sam asked, rubbing Jess' shoulder through the blankets. "Can you tell me where the thermometer is?"

"Why? I'm cold," Jess whined, burrowing her face into her pillow.

"Because you're burning up. I need to know how bad in case I have to take you to the doctor—"

"I'm fine," Jess snapped. "Just leave me be."

Sam recoiled at the venom in Jess' voice. "Okay, you rest for now. I'll be back to check on you."

The cordless sat on the kitchen table. Sam picked it up and dialed her momma's number, but the phone died on the first ring. She slammed it into the charging cradle and picked up the receiver of the phone on the wall. It crackled sporadically but rang.

"Sam? Everything okay?" Juniper picked up.

"Jess has a fever, and I don't know where the thermometer is. Would you happen to know?"

"Aveline usually keeps one in her bathroom, but if it's not there, it might've been tossed in the junk drawer. Is she okay? Do I need to come over?"

"I don't know." Sam turned to look in the direction of the stairs and froze.

A shadow cut through the small stretch of hallway between the kitchen and the living room. Malice dripped from the wispy edges of darkness. Fear slithered up Sam's spine. The shadow drew closer...

Jess stepped into the kitchen, rubbing her eyes. "Hey," she croaked. "Did you just get home?"

Sam gaped at her.

"Sam?" Juniper said on the line. "Do I need to come over?"

"N-no. I think we'll be okay. I'll call if there's any change." Sam hung up before her mother could protest. "Jess?"

Jess slumped in a chair. "Yeah?"

"Are you okay, baby?"

"I feel like shit still." She shrugged. "Why?"

"You don't remember when I came upstairs?"

"You were upstairs?"

Sam carefully closed the distance and touched Jess' forehead. Warm but not nearly as hot as before. "You have a fever. I think I should take you a doctor tomorrow."

Jess sighed and tilted her head back. "I don't want to go."

"Humor me?"

Jess huffed. "Fine."

Sam pressed a tentative kiss to Jess' temple, waiting for Jess to snap at her again. "Thank you."

"Will you get Momma to the table for me?" Jess asked, rifling through the paper bags.

"Sure, baby."

Jess smile was all teeth. Her eyes didn't crinkle at the corners. "I don't feel good, but I still have to take good care of her."

Sam couldn't shake the feeling that Jess' words were more of a threat than a comfort.

Chapter 12

Days and days of rain chased away the dredges of summer. Nights of heat lightning and dark skies finally erupted into one last thunderstorm that transitioned into several days of gray clouds and torrents of rain. The ditch filled with water. The edge of pond crept up past the willows. Sam splashed through puddles every time she had to go out to her truck which she was doing less and less, far too afraid to leave Jess for long periods of time.

Jess refused to see a doctor. Even refused to speak to Derotha when she came over. Every time Sam brought it up, Jess shut down the conversation, blaming everything on the period that wouldn't go away. It took everything for Sam not to snap in frustration. Her patience wore thin with each passing day and sleepless night.

A soft knock came from the door, barely audible over the deluge of rain. Sam craned her head over the couch and saw Celia standing on the porch, waiting for someone to unlatch the screen door so she could come in. She waved when she made eye contact with Sam.

Sam held up a finger and turned to where Jess lay in her lap, cheek smooshed against Sam's thigh, and carefully lifted up Jess' head and placed a pillow under her cheek instead. When Jess didn't stir, Sam breathed a sigh of relief. Jess only seemed to get actual sleep in these small moments and Sam didn't want to wake her.

"Hey," Sam murmured, pulling the hook out of the ring and pushing open the screen door. She stepped out onto the porch before Celia could go inside. "Mind if we talk out here a minute."

Celia shrugged. "Sure, I guess."

Sam plopped down on one of the rocking chairs and leaned back, propping her feet up on the railing.

"You look like shit, no offense," Celia said, sitting in the other chair.

Sam grunted. "Nobody fucking sleeps in this house."

"Why didn't you tell me Jess was sleepwalking again?" Celia demanded. "That's a pretty important thing to keep from me. Especially when she's supposed to be here to keep an eye on things."

"Is that why she's here?" Sam's voice was sharper than she intended, but she didn't have the energy to soften her edges.

"What the fuck does that mean?"

"It means Jess told me everything, Celia, including that you dumped her into a hospital and didn't speak to her again until you picked her up to bring her here," Sam snapped.

"Is that what she told you?" Celia huffed and ran her fingers through her hair. "I tried to tell her when I picked her up that I called nearly every single day, but they wouldn't let me talk to her. Even the lawyer iced me out when I tried to contact him. Said I had to let Jess finish her treatment without interfering or the judge could change the ruling."

Sam looked into her eyes. Looking for the telltale signs that Celia was lying. Her eyes didn't dart around wildly. The tips of her ears remained pale. She was telling the truth.

"Why wouldn't they let you speak to her?"

Celia threw up her hands. "I don't know. The nurses were always nasty to me. Said Jess was in group or in therapy or sleeping or something else. That I had no reason to contact her until her treatment was concluded. I didn't forget about her at all. I *tried* to be there when she needed me."

Sam ran her fingers through her oily hair and winced. She was so busy taking care of Jess lately that she wasn't tending to herself as much.

"You have no idea what it was like, Sam. I hadn't heard from Jess in months and all of a sudden, I get a call from her while she's in jail, telling me that she was caught trying to stab someone."

"She said she was arrested while banging on the door."

Celia shook her head. "Maybe that's how Jess wants to remember it, but I saw the evidence. She smashed through that door. If they hadn't been hiding in the other room, she might've gotten to them before the cops got to her. Jake and I had to use our savings to retain the lawyer for her, money that we were going to use to try and find a nice home for Momma so we could move her the hell out of here."

Sam let out a breath. "She told me didn't remember even going there. That she had blacked out."

"I believe she did," Celia agreed. "I always believed that, and I knew something had to have happened, but the lawyer couldn't tell me, and Jess wouldn't. But it didn't matter. They were going to put her in jail. I jumped at the chance to keep her out of there. If there was something better I could've done, please tell me, but I was just trying to keep her out of prison."

Sam didn't have anything to say. No better alternative Celia could've pursued. Sam couldn't say that she wouldn't have done anything different if the only choices were hospital or jail.

"How bad is the sleepwalking?" Celia asked, voice hushed.

"Bad."

"Shit." Celia rubbed her temples. "Has been taking her medication?"

"What medication?"

Celia scoffed. "Of-fucking-course she isn't taking it. Fuck."

"The doctors gave her something?"

Celia nodded. "They were treating Jess for bipolar disorder. Gave her medicine that was supposed to help manage the symptoms."

"I haven't seen her take anything and she never mentioned it." Sam sighed. "I don't think she's been taking it, but would it even help with the sleepwalking?"

"I don't know," Celia admitted. "How has she been otherwise?"

Sam hesitated. Should she tell Celia about Jess' rage at the fair? Would Celia rush to put Jess back into a hospital even though it clearly hadn't helped?

"She hadn't been feeling well lately, and her...she says odd things sometimes. Used to just be when I found her walking, but now she says them during the day when I think she's awake," Sam said, hedging around the whole truth.

"Like what?"

"I find her scratching around in the pantry. Talking about something under the house and in the pond. I find her in your grandfather's room all the time." Sam didn't mention the shadow she had seen, chalking that up to stress and lack of sleep. "Sometimes she talks about a baby crying. I think she's talking about the interference that comes through the monitor here and there. I've heard it too."

Celia's mouth pinched at the corners. "Under the house? The pond?"

"Ring a bell or something?"

Celia stood, crossing her arms over her chest. "Jake Jr kept saying things while we were here and on the car ride back home. I thought it was just his overactive imagination, but now..."

"Now what?" Sam pressed.

"He spoke about a man in the pond. Watching the house. Watching Auntie Jess." Celia shook her head. "What the hell does that even mean? And then he was talking about the lonely woman under the house. I...just...that can't mean anything, can it?"

Sam tapped her fingers on the arm of the chair. "I'll be honest, Cel, this house...something doesn't feel right here."

"Oh my god, please don't tell me it's haunted or anything. I mean, I grew up here. If it was haunted, I would be the first person to know."

"Maybe because it doesn't want you."

Celia scoffed. "What? It wants Jess?"

"Think about it." Sam held up her hands. "Jess started sleepwalking when we were teens, shortly after your Pawpaw died. She said she didn't sleepwalk when she lived in the city—"

Celia opened her mouth.

"Sure, she could not remember doing so while she was away, but the episodes are bad here. I mean, Christ, she woke up under the house that morning she told y'all she fell outside. Everything is worse when she's here. I don't know if it's because of memories or something more, but whatever it is, this house isn't good for her."

Celia's face crumpled. She pressed the heels of her hands to her eyes. "I don't know how to fix this, Sam. If I had my way, Momma wouldn't be here, and Jess could've stayed with me and the kids until she got back on her feet instead of being trapped here where she can't get the help she needs. What do I do?"

"You don't have to figure it out alone, Celia," Sam promised. "We can find a solution, but Jess won't get better if she stays here, that much is clear."

Celia slumped back down in the rocking chair. "I tried to so hard to manage things as best I could, and it keeps blowing up in my face."

Sam patted her hand. "There's something else. I'm not sure how to tell you."

"Oh, god."

"Your mom keeps mentioning a woman named Lottie—"

Celia stiffened.

"You know already," Sam softly accused.

"I sort of found out by accident, years ago," Celia admitted. "There's a box Momma keeps under her bed full of pictures and some letters. I was looking for anything about daddy since she never talked about him. I found out about Aunt Lottie. Momma was furious when she caught me and made me promise not to tell Jess."

"Why? Why keep your aunt from you?"

"Momma said Lottie ran away and left Momma to clean up her mess and take care of Pawpaw on her own. Part of her never forgave Lottie for that." Celia shook her head. "After that, Momma refused to talk about her again."

"Shame you never got to meet her or your cousin."

"What do you mean?"

"Darlene down at the diner told me that Lottie was pregnant when she ran away from here."

Celia's brow wrinkled. "Momma never mentioned that. Do you think she didn't know?"

"I don't know. Kind of a hard thing to hide, I'd think."

Celia pursed her lips. "I doubt she'd talk about it now."

"I haven't told Jess I know," Sam admitted. "She's been so sick that I didn't think it important right now. It won't make her feel better. But she was the one that found the chest in the attic with an old photo album with pictures of your momma and Lottie."

"A chest with just a photo album?"

"Well, no," Sam hesitated. "There was a dress, I think it was Lottie's, covered in mud or..." she trailed off, not wanting to say old, dried blood.

"Blood," Celia murmured, fingers tapping at her knees. "It was blood, wasn't it?"

"I don't know."

"Was it a child's dress?"

"I think so, why does that matter?"

Celia pressed her fingers to her mouth, her eyes looked out over the yard, blurred by the sheets of rain pouring down. "When Jess and I first had our periods, Momma took anything we bled on and tossed it into the burn pit. I remember because I always thought it was strange when we could just soak it in cold water and get rid of the stains."

"That is weird."

Celia's short laugh was devoid of humor. "I told her that and she just...I don't know...the look in her eyes always sort of haunted me. She looked so afraid and wild all at once. I thought she was going to scream at me for arguing with her. But she just gripped my shoulders so hard I couldn't move and made me promise that I wouldn't tell anyone. That if anyone but the doctor asked, I wasn't a woman yet."

"Jesus."

"Always thought it was an old-fashioned hang up that she hadn't shed from growing up feeling ashamed of her body and its functions. But there was something—I don't know what it was but there was something more in her fear. Something she wouldn't tell us."

"What do you think it was?"

Celia shrugged. "I wish I could tell you. I can barely remember growing up in this house sometimes. Memories are fuzzy or just aren't there at all. Like they don't exist or maybe I've locked them away."

"What do you remember about your grandfather?" Sam asked. "Jess hardly ever talks about him."

"Not much really. I know he lived here with us before he disappeared, but when I think of him, I don't really see anything. I couldn't even tell you what kind of person he was."

"He was a good man."

Celia and Sam both jumped. Jess stood in the open doorway. Neither of them had heard the screen door open but it sat quietly against the house. Jess' gaze zeroed in on Celia, but her face betrayed nothing but her exhaustion. If she was angry, Sam couldn't tell. Dark circles contrasted with the pale pink of her chapped lips.

"You scared the shit out of me, Jess!" Celia exclaimed, pressing her hand to her chest. "Are you alright?"

"He was a good man," Jess repeated hollowly. "He loved us."

"Oh, well that's—"

"But I was his favorite," Jess interrupted Celia. "You were always jealous that he gave me more attention than he gave you. Momma was the same about Lottie—"

"Who told you about Lottie?" Sam asked, standing up from her chair.

"Pawpaw did."

Celia blinked, mouth hanging open. "Jess, what on earth are you talking about? Pawpaw has been gone, he's probably dead. He couldn't have told you about Lottie."

"He tells me things. Whispers them to me."

"What? When?" When Jess didn't answer, Sam reached for her hand, but Jess recoiled, her lip curling in disgust. "Jess?"

"You should go home, Sam," Jess said. "Family is visiting today. You're not family."

Celia shot up. "Jess!"

Sam's gut twisted. This wasn't Jess, couldn't be Jess, but the words were a knife digging into Sam's heart all the same. "Jess, you're not feeling well. You need rest—"

"I don't need anything from you," Jess snapped. "It's pathetic you're still clinging to me after all these years, too scared to move on and burden someone else. Fuck, you can't even move out of a town that hates your guts. Your parents can't even go to their own church anymore because of you. You've made them pariahs and you're trying to do the same to me. Is that really love, Sam?"

Sam choked on her reply. Tears welled in her eyes. How could Jess say these things? Why was she saying these things?

The sound of rain covered Celia's palm cracking against Jess' cheek. Jess touched the blooming pink welt spreading across her face. Pure rage filled her eyes as she turned her gaze on Celia and Celia stumbled back, bumping into Sam. But Jess just smiled.

"I was just kidding," she said, voice syrupy sweet. "But you should go home, Sam. I want to spend some time with Celia and Momma. You've been taking such good care of me, baby. You deserve a break."

She didn't wait for a response. Jess walked back into the house and straight up the stairs. They watched her open the door to her grandfather's room and step inside, the door slamming shut so hard the whole house reverberated.

"What the fuck," Celia mumbled.

Sam covered her quivering mouth. "What the fuck do we do?"

"Honestly? She either needs an ass whooping or an exorcism and I'm not entirely sure which one yet." Celia scrubbed her hand down her face. "But maybe you should go home for a bit. Get some rest at least."

"I'm not sure I want to leave," Sam admitted, though she didn't know if she could handle more biting remarks from Jess, false or not.

"I know." Celia touched her elbow. "But you're hanging on by a thread here. Have you even gone to work lately?"

Sam hadn't gone for the last few days with Keith's blessing, worried that something might happen when she left. A worry that she couldn't shake now even though Celia was here.

"I'm going to stay. Try to talk to her and Momma. I don't know if it will change anything, but it'll give you a chance to recharge." Celia propped her hands on her hips. "Go see your Ma. Maybe she'll know how to handle Jess. She used to handle us all the time as kids."

Juniper might know how best to handle Jess. Maybe even be the only one able to talk Jess into going to a doctor or a hospital. And there was something that had been bothering Sam for days. Something she wanted to talk to both of her parents about but especially her father. Darlene's words kept looping in her head.

He was sweet on her all those years ago. Pretty sure he planned on marrying her even though, rumor has it, the baby wasn't his.

Keith had never once mentioned Lottie while Sam was growing up, and she couldn't imagine why no one talked about her. Sure, maybe Aveline was bitter and that was why, but if Keith loved her like he said, why hadn't he mentioned her even once? Sam felt like there was something else. A secret they were keeping.

"I'll go visit with Ma for a bit, but I'll be back tonight," Sam promised. "If you need anything—"

Celia waved her hand. "I'll call, I promise. I was planning on spending the night so coming back tonight is completely up to you."

"I'll be back."

Sam grabbed her keys from the hook by the door, her yellow rain jacket, and jogged out to her truck. Celia remained on the porch, a blurry shadow in the rain. Everything in Sam screamed not to leave Jess behind. That they should drag her out of that house kicking and screaming. Sam never really believed in haunted houses or ghosts growing up. She always thought hauntings were people manifesting their own grief and guilt about losing loved ones.

But now she wasn't sure at all.

She had seen things in that house. Heard things. Then there was Jess' behavior. How many things could she chalk up to happenstance before she was branded a fool? Too scared to face the truth of things.

The rain wasn't as harsh as she drove down the wooded path to her parents' house. Everyone was home, all cars lined up in a row. Sam pulled in beside Lily's car and hopped out, running through the mud to the porch. Hound napped on the other side of the screen, happy he had been let inside to stay dry so long as he stayed out of the kitchen, and slowly stood up to stretch while Sam kicked off her muddy boots on the porch.

Juniper looked up from the blue floral couch, her reading glasses perched on the edge of her nose and a magazine open in her lap. Keith sat in his recliner, enamored with the court show playing on TV, holding a cup of coffee in one hand and a remote in the other.

"Oh hey, hun, is Jess feeling better?" Juniper asked.

Sam sank down beside Juniper. Hound's tail lashed her knees until Hound turned and placed his head in Sam's lap. The tears came quick. Unbidden. The stress of the last few weeks poured down her face.

"Oh, dear." Juniper set the magazine aside and rubbed Sam's back. "Did something happen?"

Keith muted the television and set down his cup. "Is something wrong with Jess?"

The words poured out as quickly as the tears. Sam unloaded everything she had kept to herself. The sleepwalking. Jess' behavior. The hurtful barbs she had just thrown at Sam to get her to leave. Sam's worry that Jess actually meant them.

"Oh, darlin', why didn't you tell us any of this before?" Juniper murmured, brushing her fingers through Sam's hair. "Listen, I don't know what's going on with Jess, but what she said about us isn't true. We aren't pariahs, and we left the church of our own volition."

"Always wanted to after that prick started preachin'," Keith grunted.

Juniper hissed his name and shook her head. "Your father is right even though I don't approve of his language. We weren't fond of him when we were growing up, and even less so now." She curled her fingers under Sam's chin and wiped away Sam's tears with her other hand. "When he allowed people to say nasty things about you, we finally made the choice to leave. A church should never allow hate in its walls. That's not what our Lord stands for, and it's not what we will stand for either."

"We don't need a church to worship," Keith added.

"No, we don't," Juniper agreed.

"I just don't understand why she would say those things to me," Sam whispered. "I thought she loved me."

"I'm not certain about many things, but I am certain that Jess loves you," Keith added. "That was true when you was kids and it's true now. Something else is going on."

Juniper nodded. "I agree. Now we know Jess was in the hospital before she came here—"

"You knew," Sam said, looking between them. "Why didn't you tell me?"

"We didn't think it right," Keith answered.

"We thought Jess should be the one to tell you," Juniper added. "And it sounds as though she did."

"But what's happening now...I don't think it's related. I think..." Sam hesitated. "I think whatever is happening, has something to do with Lottie."

Juniper froze, wide eyes flitting briefly to Keith's. "Who...why would you think this has something to do with Lottie? How do you even know about her?"

"Aveline mentions her sometimes but wouldn't tell us who she is. Jess found a chest with photos of her and a bloody dress—"

Juniper leaned away and held her hand to her mouth.

"I saw the picture at the diner." Sam looked at Keith. "The one you're in with her. Darlene told me you were sweet on her before she disappeared."

"I told Darlene to take that shit down," Keith grumbled.

"Why? What happened to Lottie? Why doesn't anyone talk about—"

"Stop right there," Keith's voice dropped, growling in a way Sam had never heard before though she had seen her father get mad plenty of times. "We are not talking about Lottie in this house."

"Why?"

Keith stood and pointed a thick finger at Sam. "I'm telling you, Sam, leave it alone. Lottie is none of your damn concern."

"Was the baby yours?"

Keith crossed the room, arm outstretched as if to reach for Sam's collar. "How dare—"

Juniper jumped up and held her hand out. "Enough!"

Keith stopped, chest heaving, eyes blazing with anger.

She slowly sank back down on the couch beside Sam. "No, Lottie's baby was not your father's."

"Juney," Keith said her name as a warning, but nothing else came out. If Juniper was bound to answer, there was nothing he could do to stop her. He slumped down in his recliner and held his head in his hands.

"Your father did court her, well before we were ever together. Aveline and Lottie weren't allowed to date by their father. It was the worst, best kept secret. Everyone in town knew, but everyone knew better than to mention it to their father." Juniper briefly closed her eyes. "He was an awful man. Folks were afraid of him. Those girls were afraid."

"Juney, please," Keith pleaded.

"It's better it comes from us," Juniper whispered. "Better from us than someone who will twist the truth."

"What truth?" Sam asked.

"Lottie was meant to meet your father at the fair one night. Aveline was supposed to wait with her, but she left Lottie alone when her date arrived early." Juniper drew in a shaky breath. "No one saw those men go after her and drag her into the woods."

"I waited for hours. I thought she couldn't sneak away," Keith's voice was muffled by his hands. "I don't know how she got home that night, but Aveline told me everything when Lottie stopped showing up to meet us. She refused to see me. We were both ashamed for very different reasons."

"When did you find out about the baby?" Sam sniffed.

"She called me late one night. Panicked. Told me she was pregnant, and she was terrified of what might happen when her father found out." Keith finally sat up, eyes rimmed with red. "We were almost ready to graduate. I told her I'd propose. Ask her daddy properly and whisk her away before he found out. I promised I'd take care of her and the baby like they were my own."

"Why didn't you?"

Keith's shoulders shook. "I went there to talk to him. Had a ring and everything. She opened the door." Keith stopped and rubbed his eyes. "I'll never forget the look in her eyes. As if she had been hollowed out. Every bit of light had vanished. She told me it wasn't necessary anymore. That I had to leave."

"And you did?"

"Not at first," Keith chuckled darkly. "But staring down the barrel of her daddy's shotgun had me hauling ass back home."

Juniper stood and crossed the room to rub Keith's back. "Nobody saw much of Lottie for months. Aveline would pop into town for things, but she didn't talk about Lottie. Didn't talk about anything that happened in that house until one day she started walking around with two little girls, almost school age by then, telling folks she had hidden her pregnancies, and no one heard from Lottie again."

"No," Sam mumbled. "That's not..."

"Sam—"

Sam shook her head. "You can't be telling me that Celia and Jess are—it's just not possible. They can't be Lottie's...can they? That would make them twins. They don't even look alike!"

"We had our suspicions but couldn't prove anything. Even the birth certificates lists Jess' birth date occurring nearly a year after Celia's. But Aveline's father was also a good friend of Reverend Michael's, and that man held a lot of sway with the right people." Juniper perched on the arm of the recliner. "I know this is a lot to take in—"

"How do you even know this for sure if Aveline never admitted—"

"She did, years later," Keith whispered. "When she called that night and told me what she done."

Juniper closed her eyes.

Sam clasped her hands in her lap, almost too afraid to ask even though she was finally getting the full picture. "What had she done?"

"Now, you have to understand what kind of bastard her daddy was," Keith said. "He was cruel. Never hesitant to raise a hand to those girls. Kept an iron grip on them. Considered them *his*."

"There were always rumors about what happened in that house," Juniper kept her voice hushed as if she were afraid someone might overhear them in their own house. "Whispers about what he did to his girls treated as church gossip. A warning lesson to other kids, that they could have *him* as their father instead of their own parents."

Keith's hands shook. He balled them into fists so tight the knuckles turned white.

"Aveline raised those girls like they were hers, but she couldn't shake her father's shadow. Couldn't walk away from him no matter how much she wanted to." Juniper swallowed. "Until she found...until..."

Sam didn't think she wanted to hear anymore.

"She locked the girls in their room and bashed his head in with a cast iron," Keith said, cutting Juniper off. "Best damn thing she ever did if you ask me."

Juniper didn't disagree.

"And she called you that night. That's the night you brought the girls over, and Ma told us their grandpa hadn't come home from a hunting trip and you were going to look for him," Sam guessed.

"I'm surprised you remember that," Juniper said.

"Yes," Keith answered. "We brought the girls here so I could help Aveline clean it up. We took care of the body and cleaned the place so no one would ever question her. Lucky for her, the only person who gave a shit about that man was on his deathbed."

Sam's knee jiggled. She twisted her fingers together. Juniper had it right. This was a lot to take in at once.

"What happened to Lottie?" Sam choked out.

"Aveline said she was there one night and gone the next morning. Left a note that she had run off," Juniper said. "No one knows."

"The bastard killed her," Keith muttered darkly.

"More than likely," Juniper quietly agreed, reaching for Keith's hand and gently unfurling his fingers.

Sam ran her fingers through her hair, tugging at the strands, the tiny shocks of pain keeping her from completely losing it. "You're sure he's dead."

"If he wasn't, he was when we sank him in the pond."

A man in the pond, watching the house, watching Jess.

"Oh, god," Sam choked, shooting up to her feet and running for the phone.

"Sam?" Juniper asked, rising from the recliner. "Something the matter?"

The receiver nearly jumped out of Sam's hands as she ripped it off the cradle. "When Jess sleepwalks she sometimes talks about something in the pond, something under the house, babies crying—" Sam broke off to fit the receiver to her ear and heard Lily on the other end. "Lily get off the damn phone!"

"Stop listening in!" Lily shrieked, heard both on the phone and upstairs in her room.

Sam slammed the receiver back into the cradle and Lily howled.

Juniper held up her hands. "It may not mean anything. They could just be dreams."

Sam picked up the phone and the line was clear. "No, you don't understand. He's trying to take her."

"Sam, he's dead—"

"I know that!" Sam yelled and Juniper's head snapped back in surprise. "But I've seen things in that house. I've heard things. Shadows standing over her. Babies crying on the monitor. And before I left here, she was saying shit like she was his favorite just like Lottie was his favorite."

"Oh, Christ in heaven," Juniper gasped, quickly crossing herself, and turned to Keith. "That...she couldn't..."

Sam punched in Jess' number. The line trilled in her ear as she tapped her foot. The line clicked after the fourth ring. "Celia? Jess? It's me Sam, look—"

Gurgling breaths filled the line and the words died on Sam's lips. She held the receiver away from her ear, the breaths so loud that even Juniper and Keith could hear them clear across the room.

"Hello?" Sam whispered.

"STAY AWAY!"

The line went dead. Sam punched in the number over and over, but the phone wouldn't even ring.

"I-I have to go get her," Sam whimpered.

Juniper grasped her arm. "You're not going alone."

Chapter 13

BRACKISH SWEAT DRIPPED FROM Jess' hairline, sluicing down her face and neck and turning the collar of her tank top from white to brown. She wiped away drop after drop, but she was too hot. Muggy air clung to her skin. Suffocating her. Jess sat back on the couch, her feet crossed on the table in front of her, hoping for a scrap of air from the window unit by Momma's chair. Celia sat on the other end of the couch, wrinkling her nose.

Thunder rumbled in the distance. The rain hadn't stopped for hours, darkening the sky when it was barely evening.

"Where's Sam," Jess grumbled, staring blankly at the TV. She had been staring at the screen for a while but could honestly say she had no idea what was going on. Her brain felt fuzzy. Foggy. Had she taken the medicine? Would she remember if she had?

"You sent her away, remember?" Celia sneered; her arms crossed over her chest. "Said some pretty awful things to your girlfriend."

"What did you say to Sam?" Aveline demanded.

"I didn't say anything," Jess whined. "I haven't even seen her since this morning."

"Jesus, you don't even remember, do you?" Celia griped.

"Remember what?"

"Telling her she was a burden to everyone around her. That she was pathetic for still loving you after all these years," Celia answered. "She's not pathetic for still loving you but fuck she just might be a glutton for punishment."

"What horrible things to say." Aveline clicked her tongue against her teeth. "You're really a terrible girl, Jess. I tried my best with you, but I don't even think God can fix the ugliness in your heart."

"W-what?" Jess croaked. "How could you say that about me?"

"It's no secret daddy left because of you," Celia taunted. "He just couldn't handle you. Your rages. Your destruction. You destroy everything you touch. Suppose it's better you sent Sam away now before you destroy her too."

"But I don't," Jess argued, tears brimming. "I don't destroy everything. Why are you saying these things to me?"

Celia shrugged. "It's what we really think of you. Why should we keep hiding it?"

"You have to realize how bad you are, Jess," Aveline added. "Bad apple spoils the bunch as Pa used to say. Maybe you should go. Run far away again. Maybe you'll be worth something when you come back again."

"And you'll come back," Celia said.

"You just can't make it on your own." Aveline shook her head.

"Not staying on her feet anyway," Celia snickered. "Always eager to open your legs if you get ahead, right Jess?"

Aveline laughed with her.

"Stop it." Jess' voice shook. "I'm...I'm not—"

"A slut?" Celia drawled.

"A floozy?" Aveline said.

Jess' arms shook as she tried to push herself up. "Knock it off."

"Oh, look Ma, she's mad," Celia mocked. "Think she's going to beat me into a pulp and pretend she had a good reason for it?"

"More than likely."

Jess swallowed a sob. "Leave me alone."

"Why don't you hit me then, crybaby."

"Stop it!" Jess yelled, shoving herself to her feet.

The floor tipped under her feet. She stumbled forward, throwing her hands up for when she tripped over the table and fell to the floor. Gravel bit into her hands. The thin rocks shredded her knee. She burst into tears, watching the droplets of blood drip down her leg.

"Poor Jessamine. Are those boys picking on you again?"

Pawpaw crouched beside her, hand curling around her knee to look at the damage. His dark eyes crinkled in the corner as he smiled at her. "It's not so bad. No need to cry darlin'."

"They won't stop pushing me," Jess hiccuped through her words. "They're always mean to me. Telling me girls isn't allowed. And they pull my hair."

Pawpaw gently tugged one of her pigtails. "Remember what I taught you last time? How to ball your hand into a fist?"

She nodded.

"Next time they pick on you, hit them back. Hit them hard." He twirled her hair around his finger. "Hit them over and over again. Don't ever let them think you're weak, you understand?"

"Yes, Paw." She sniffed.

He smiled crookedly. "Good girl. Now give your Pawpaw a kiss and go play."

Jess darted forward and kissed his wrinkled cheek before running off with a giggle.

Grass tickled her legs. Bugs clung to the hem of her skirt. Jess ran circles around the house chasing dragonflies as they darted from her

hands and fled to the pond. Her hands slammed closed over an irides-
cent body. Wings fluttered uselessly against her palms. She watched it
struggle in her grasp.

"Jessamine?" a soft voice called from the dark opening to the crawlspace. "Baby, is that you?"

Her hands fell away and the dragonfly darted to safety. The darkness of the opening called to her. Jess crept closer. She knelt down in
the grass and gripped the bricks, wriggling her head and shoulders inside. Weeds poked out of the dirt, tiny purple flowers and fuzzy white
dandelions. Movement in the corner of her eye drew her attention.

A dark figure crouched in the corner. Thin limbs caked in mud
and sprinkled with dirt twitched. A gaunt face peered at her, detritus ground into the lines of their skin. Thick dark hair, matted and
muddy, hung down to their naked waist. A soft sob fell from their lips,
flashing yellowed and missing teeth, before they pressed their mouth
closed.

"Jess," they croaked, reaching out with a gnarled hand. "Baby, it's
me. It's Momma."

"My momma's in the house," Jess said. "I don't think she would
like me talking to a stranger."

They moved closer, crawling towards her. They jerked as something
tugged at their ankle. A thin line in the dirt looked like a snake following the person's foot.

Rusted chains twined around brick under the house.

Jess tilted her head. "What's your name, ma'am or sir?"

"M-my name?"

"Momma said it's polite to ask people their names, and I should
always address them respectfully or she'll have to put me over her
knee." Jess leaned her elbows on the brick. "And if you tell me your

name, you're not a stranger anymore and I can talk to you. That way I'm not breaking Momma's rules."

"Lottie," they answered, voice cracking. "I'm Lottie. I'm...I—"

"Nice to meet you, Miss Lottie. Why are you under our house? Do you live here?"

"I—"

"Jessamine!"

Jess looked over her shoulder right as Momma's claws dug into her shoulder and pulled her out of the opening. Momma's eyes were wide and fearful. She yanked Jess to her feet.

"I was just talking to Miss Lottie, Momma—"

Momma's palm thundered against her cheek. Jess choked back a cry and tried to stumble away but Momma kept a grip on her shoulder.

"Please, Aveline," Lottie wailed and sobbed from under the house. "I just want to see my babies. I said I was sorry!"

"Shut up!" Momma shrieked at the opening and turned back to Jess. "You are to never go near there again; do you understand me?"

"B-but—"

"Never again, Jessamine!"

"Aveline," Pawpaw's voice was calm. "Let Jessamine go. You're scaring her."

Aveline's hands shook as she unfurled her fingers from the fabric of Jess' dress. Her eyes didn't meet Pawpaw's. "I'm sorry, Daddy, but she—"

Pawpaw held up a hand. "Incidents happen, Aveline. Why don't you take Jessamine in to play with Celia before you make dinner."

"What about Miss Lottie?" Jess demanded.

Aveline sucked in a breath, but Pawpaw just smiled. "I'm going to take good care of Miss Lottie, I promise."

Jess held up her pinky and he hooked his pinky around hers. "You can't break your promise, Paw."

"I never do, darlin'."

"You could promise to take me swimming later too," Jess added with a sly smile.

"How can I say no to my favorite girl?" He stood up and looked at Aveline, eyes going hard. "Take her inside, Aveline."

Without needing to be told again, Aveline scooped Jess into her arms and carried her around the house as fast as she could, but Jess still heard Lottie's desperate scream.

"Why is Lottie down there, Momma?"

Aveline's arms were a trembling vise. "That's where little girls who don't listen go, baby."

"Are you going to put me down there?"

Aveline choked back a sob. "No, honey. Never. You're never going down there so long as you're good for Pa. Just be good, okay?"

"I'll be good," Jess promised.

Aveline's arms fell away. Jess fell, bouncing against a soft mattress. Darkness danced over the ceiling. Heat clung to her skin, but she shivered from the bitter cold seeping into her bones. Sweat beaded on her upper lip. She coughed, spitting brackish water from her mouth. Fingers that didn't belong to her brushed over her lips.

"My poor Jessamine." The bed dipped beside her. Pawpaw's fingers moved through her hair, pulling it away from her face. "Not feeling well are you, darlin'?"

She slowly shook her head, her temples throbbing and the pulsating behind her eyes growing agonizing with each second. Bile lingered in her throat as her stomach roiled and threatened to spill its contents. She didn't think she had anything left in her. There was a hollowness, as if someone had cut her open and scooped everything out, leaving behind an empty cavity. Jess didn't think she could ever feel better not so long as she was empty.

"You're in so much pain," he cooed, fingers squelching against her cheek. "Everyone hurts you, even the people who are supposed to love you for who you are. They turn their backs when you need them. Lock you away when you're too much for them. Envious of how special you are."

"Sam," she mumbled.

"Isn't here," Pawpaw reminded her. "Left you alone with your mother and sister who don't love you at all. They say terrible things about you. Behind your back. To your face."

"No," Jess protested weakly, haze crowding her mind. She couldn't remember why Sam wasn't here, but Sam wouldn't just leave her alone for no reason. Sam loved her.

"But she doesn't," Pawpaw said. "She doesn't really love you. She used to. Took what you gave her and squandered it. She isn't worthy of you, Jessamine. None of them are."

Jess blinked, eyes struggling to stay open.

"I've always loved exactly as you are, my girl," he promised. "You believe me, don't you?"

Jess nodded.

"Good. Now, I owe my favorite girl a swim."

"I'm sick," Jess muttered.

"You'll feel better, I promise."

Jess held up a shaking pinky. Loamy flesh curled around her pinky. Thick, ooze dripped down her hand.

"I promise," Pawpaw said. "Now take my hand."

Freezing cold hands grasped hers. The skin around his fingers was thick and bloated. He intertwined their fingers and clutched her palm against his. The door to his room creaked open and he slowly led her into the darkened hallway. Light flickered from the bottom of the stairs, a beacon for her to follow as she clung to the wall with her other hand and shakily walked downstairs.

Celia sat on the couch, head tilted back and mouth slightly open. A soft snore escaped her lips. A cold empty cup sat on the table in front of her. Jess paused at the bottom of the stairs.

"Can Celia come?" she asked.

"You didn't want Celia to come, remember?" he said. "You made her sleep because you wanted to spend time with me by yourself."

"I did?"

Pawpaw tugged her towards the kitchen.

Aveline whimpered from her recliner. Jess craned her head to look over her shoulder. Momma sat in her recliner, eyes wide and staring at the shadow that leaned over her, dark hair dripping dirt and mud into Momma's lap. The darkness shifted, turning its head to watch Jess as she followed Pawpaw into the yard. A loud wail was cut off by the kitchen door slamming shut.

Grass tickled her ankles as Pawpaw led her down the gentle slope of the backyard. Crying came from the opening to the crawlspace. Jess watched as thin arms reached out, fingers clawing at the brick, the crying growing louder and louder into familiar screaming.

"Wake up, baby, please!" Lottie shrieked. "Please! Please!"

Jess turned away.

Water lapped at her ankles, warm like bathwater, and she sighed. Silt squished between her toes. Fish darted around her legs, scales brushing against her skin. Pawpaw tugged her in, deeper and deeper, dark water soaking into her shorts and then her tank top. Gentle waves teased her belly.

"Jess!" Sam's voice rang out, pushing through the fog.

Jess jolted. "Sam?"

"No," Pawpaw growled. "She left you, Jessamine. Don't forget that."

Jess tried to turn away, but Pawpaw pulled her further in. "I want to go back," she gasped. "I want to see Sam."

Bloated fingers grasped her neck. Pawpaw turned Jess back to face him. To see him. Really see him. The bloated, rotted thing that used to be her grandfather. His grip on her throat killed her scream.

"It'll be over soon, my girl, I promise." He patted her cheek. "And I never break my promises, do I?"

He plunged her under the water.

Keith broke every speed limit, racing through the rain to Jess' house. The clouds grew thicker. Lightning lit up the sky, racing between the dark masses. Sam sat in the backseat with Lily—who had no idea what was going on other than 'Jess is in trouble' and didn't hesitate to climb into the truck behind them—hitting her fist against her knee.

She would never forgive herself if something happened to Jess while she was gone.

Keith slammed the truck into park behind Celia's car in the driveway and they piled out of the truck. The house was dim. Not even the porch light shone like a beacon in the thick dark. Sam didn't bother knocking. She flung open the front door and barreled inside, preparing herself for the worst.

Flashing lights lit up Celia's slackened face. She snored, her head tilted back and her mouth hanging open. Aveline sat in her chair, but she wasn't asleep. She twisted her fingers together, sobbing softly, cheeks glistening in the television's glare.

"Aveline?" Juniper rushed in. "Why are you crying?"

"I'm s-sorry," Aveline cried. "I'm so sorry."

"Did something happen? Where's Jess?" Sam demanded.

Aveline kept crying and rocking in her chair.

Sam ran upstairs, throwing open every single door, but Jess wasn't upstairs. "She's not up here!" she called down, boots thudding down the stairs.

"She's not down here," Keith met Sam at the bottom of the stairs. "All the doors leading to outside are shut tight."

Juniper gently shook Celia, but she didn't stir.

"Come look at this," Lily called from the kitchen.

They crowded into the kitchen, leaving Aveline sobbing alone in her chair. Sam couldn't stop to help her. Not until she knew Jess was okay.

Lily held up an opened brown bottle. The cap lay on the counter next to a cold kettle and a box of tea. "I think Jess drugged Celia."

Juniper snatched the bottle. "God, how many do you think she used?"

"Just get her into her car and drive her to the county hospital! We have to find Jess before..." Keith trailed off. "The pond."

"What?" Lily said, looking around confused.

"We sank him in the pond," he whispered.

Sam didn't think. She ripped open the kitchen door and raced onto the muddy grass. Two dark figures stood chest-deep in the water. She knew in her heart one of them was Jess.

"Jess!" she screamed, voice whisked away by the wind.

But Jess turned her head. Fixed Sam with wide, terrified eyes. And then she was gone. There one moment, pulled under the water next.

"No!"

Mud sucked at her boots. Roots snagged her ankle. The pond telling Sam: *She's ours now. Turn back.* But Sam wouldn't let the water have Jess. Not ever. She dove under, legs kicking and thrashing, propelling her forward. Her eyes stung but she couldn't close them. Her fingers reached, searching wildly.

Her heart leapt out of her chest when she brushed Jess' fingers. Bubbles burst against her face. A silent scream. Jess clawed Sam's wrists, trying to hold on as something pulled her further into the lake. Sam hooked her arms under Jess' arms and swam backwards. They both jerked. Jess tried to move her leg, but it wouldn't budge.

There wasn't much time. Jess' scream had cost her precious air. Sam felt her way down Jess' body, hands sliding over thighs, searching for what was keeping her there. Skeletal fingers wrapped around Jess' ankles. Sam tugged at them, but they wouldn't let go.

Jess' legs slowed.

Sam grasped the wrist attached and pulled with all of her might. If she couldn't make it let go, then she was bringing it with her. The skeleton pulled free of the muck at the bottom. Dirt swirled, rising up with the remains. Jess had stopped moving. Her eyes were closed, chest still.

Panic punched its way into Sam's chest and throttled her heart, but she didn't stop. She grasped Jess with one hand and desperately paddled to shore.

Water splashed as Keith ran in, pulling Jess out and dragging her limp body past the shore and onto the grass, the upper torso of a skeleton still attached to her ankle. Sam crawled out after her, mud gathering under her nails as she pulled herself up beside Jess.

Jess didn't breathe. Didn't move. Sam pressed fingers to her neck, feeling the sluggish pulse. One hand on top of the other, she pushed on

Jess' chest, counting under her breath. She stopped and leaned down, pinching Jess' nose shut and breathing air into her lungs.

"Come on, baby, please," Sam begged, pumping Jess' chest once more. "You can't leave me. I just got you back again."

"You can do it, Jess," Keith nearly sobbed, something he never did, and brushed damp hair from her face. "Come back to us."

Jess coughed. Water burst from her lips and splattered against' Sam's face. She didn't damn well care. A relieved sob shuddered through her body, and she pulled Jess into her lap, rubbing her back as Jess spat water onto the grass.

"Oh, thank God." Keith rubbed his hand down his face. "I'm so sorry, Jess."

Jess shivered, clawing at Sam's sleeves. Her eyes darted around wildly as if she didn't know where she was. Air rattled in her throat. She'd need a doctor. Someone to check her lungs and make sure she had retched up all the water. After that...well, they would just have to take things one day at a time. Sam wouldn't leave her. Never. She would get Jess what she needed, and she would stay. Here or anywhere else.

"I have you, baby, I promise," Sam whispered, clutching Jess in her arms. "You're safe."

Jess' eyes landed on the opening in the crawlspace. She held up a shaking hand, pointing or reaching, Sam couldn't tell. A soft cry fell from her lips. Tears rolled down her cheeks and clung onto the tip of her nose.

"Jess?" Sam stroked her cheek. "Does something hurt? What's wrong?"

"L-lot," she croaked, trying to force the words out.

"Don't hurt yourself, hun'," Keith fussed. "Whatever you're trying to say can wait."

"L-Lottie," Jess whispered.

"Lottie? What about Lottie?" Keith asked, earlier words forgotten.

Jess pointed to the crawlspace again. "There."

Keith paled. "Oh, God. No." A sob burst from his lips. "No, no."

Jess turned her face into Sam's stomach and wailed.

Chapter 14

PINK PETALS DANCED IN the breeze and tickled her cheeks as the wind whispered through the perfectly lined trees. Jess breathed in the sweet, perfumed air, thick with eastern redbuds and magnolia trees surrounding the still lake. A man-made lake, but calm and beautiful all the same. She walked along the smooth concrete path that curved around the water, nodding softly with a smile at people walking in the opposite direction. Children darted amongst the trees, playing tag or whatever imaginary game their minds had conjured up. Local college students played frisbee on the stretches of green and held study groups at the picnic benches. Mothers with strollers and elderly folks with canes, rested on the stone benches spaced along the trail. Most of them barely noticed her presence—just another face walking through the park—and those that did, didn't look at her with contempt or derision.

This was what she loved about living in the city. Being another nobody in a sea of nobodies. Though she hadn't been here for long, Jess felt as if she could breathe again.

She readjusted the strap of her crossbody bag, her thumb hooking around the strap, and strayed from the trail. Soft grass cradled her boots. Ladybugs crawled across blades of grass. Jess paused to gently pick one off her boot and place it back on the green. Two magnolias sat side by side, their branches growing into each other and tangling together like lovers, with just enough space for Jess to walk through and take a set of steps to a wrought iron gate. She fished through her pack for her employee card and slid it through the card reader. The red light flashed, and she huffed, slowly sliding it one more time. She had complained to maintenance about the finicky machine, but they weren't in any hurry to replace it.

Lacey Retirement Home had once been the Caldwell Home for the Mentally Disturbed and before that had been a family home for a ship captain who transported slaves into the local port, his blood money netting him a large plot of land and a grand home where his wife and five children—all but two had succumbed to a wasting sickness—had lived in relative comfort to the suffering they took part in. Three stories. Huge grounds with a garden the patients tended, and more recently, a shuffleboard court. A wraparound porch littered with rocking chairs. Jess jogged up to the steps where Loretta, a middle-aged nurse with deep lines and several gray hairs, sat with a cigarette dangling from her lips.

"I thought you were off today?" Loretta rasped, digging in her bright pink scrubs for her lighter.

Jess paused by the railing, one foot on the first step. "I am. Just came by to visit Momma. How is she today?"

"Caused quite a bit of fuss this morning. Not entirely her fault, mind. She whooped Mr. Reed at cards, and he was a bit of a sore loser." Loretta chuckled, pulling the cigarette from her lips. "He was too busy flirting to know he had been had."

Jess giggled. "Good. Maybe he'll stop sniffing around then."

"Trust me, darlin', if it's not him it'll be some other rooster strutting about."

"I hope not. I'd hate to have to give Momma 'the talk.'" Jess shuddered. "To be honest, I didn't expect there to be this much sex going on in an old folk's home."

Loretta guffawed. "They may be old, hun, but they ain't dead yet!"

The screen door creaked open and one of the day janitors, Vicky, stepped out onto the back porch with a red Slim Jim lunchbox—her son's more than likely—and a thermos of coffee. Cigarettes poked out of the top of the pocket sewed into her baby blue uniform shirt.

"I thought you were off today?" she echoed, popping a squat next to Loretta on the steps. "Or did Nick call you in since Ida called off?"

"Ida called off?" Jess leaned against the railing. "He didn't call me in. I'm just here to see Momma. I work tomorrow though."

Vicky set her lunchbox on her knees and opened it, unwrapping a peanut butter and jelly sandwich. "Any chance you could come in an hour early tomorrow? I gotta take Luis to an appointment and Alex can't pick him up from school for me."

"Is he sick?"

"Nah, just a check-up, but he wants to sign-up for a community baseball league, and they need to know he's fine to play. If I don't take him now, he might not make it to sign-ups." She took a bite of her sandwich, peanut butter lingering in the crease of her mouth. "I'd rather him stay busy this summer than hang out with those kids around Shipyard."

"Luis is a good kid."

"And I want him to stay that way."

Loretta huffed, giving up on her search for her lighter and turning to Vicky. "Can I borrow your lighter."

"Well, I'm going to go see Momma before it gets too late," Jess said.

"She's on the front porch last I checked," Loretta offered, finally lighting her cigarette and taking a drag.

"Thanks."

Jess took the porch around to the front of the old Victorian just in case Nick was inside and decided to ask her to cover the night shift. While Jess didn't mind the work as much as she thought she would when she took the job, she hated working overnight. Most of the shift was spent doing laundry and emergency clean-ups but the problem was the dark that lingered too long in corners and the creak of footsteps on the floors above when everyone was supposedly asleep. The new meds her therapist had prescribed helped with most of her anxieties but there were times when Jess was back in her childhood home, spectral hands digging into her skin and guiding her through mud to the waiting water. Working at night exacerbated those episodes, so she stuck to her day shifts.

Momma gently rocked back in forth in a white rocking chair, crochet hooks clicking as she looped lavender yarn around the hooks into a loose shape that sat in a heap on her lap. A blanket, if Jess had to guess. Aveline hummed softly in the gentle silence of the afternoon.

There were many things Jess didn't remember about that last night in the house. She didn't remember dumping her medication into Celia's tea, thankfully most of the pills spilled onto the counter and the floor, and waiting for her sister to pass out. Hell, she barely remembered walking out into the lake and nearly drowning. And what she did remember, she sorely wished she hadn't. Memories had slithered out of the box she kept them in, and they wouldn't go back in no matter how she wished. Even with therapy, Jess still had plenty of nightmares.

"Are you going to stand there and stare at me, Jessamine?" Aveline said, her voice clearer than it had ever been at the house.

Once Aveline had left the house, first spending time in the county hospital and then some time at the Williams' house while Celia and

Jess searched for an affordable care home, she slowly got better. There were things she would never get back, but she had more good days than bad.

Jess crossed the porch and sat in the rocking chair beside her mother. "What are you making, Momma?"

"A blanket for little Abby. It's her birthday this weekend, isn't it?"

Jess nodded. "It is. Do you know how old she's going to be?"

Aveline side-eyed her. "Are you asking because you don't know or are you testing my memory today, Jessamine?"

Jess grinned sheepishly.

Aveline scoffed but there was no bite to it. No disappointment seeded in the huff of breath and shake of her head. "She's going to be three. And her birthday is actually tomorrow, but Celia is bringing the kids on Saturday to celebrate."

Jess leaned back in her chair. "I'm glad you remember, Momma. Honestly."

"I know." Aveline sighed and set the yarn down in her lap. "I know none of this has been easy on you or Celia. This whole entire mess. I..." she trailed off, a stray tear slipping down her wizened cheek.

Jess reached out, hesitating for only a brief moment, and rested her hand on top of Aveline's. "It's alright, Momma."

Aveline shook her head. "I knew...I knew she hadn't really left. I knew he had lied to me, but I was..." she choked on the words.

"We don't blame you for that," Jess promised, squeezing her mother's hand.

There were many things to blame Aveline for. The sharp barbs she constantly threw at Jess. Punishing Jess—even if she didn't know she was doing it—just because Jess reminded her so much of Lottie. Those things Jess would blame her mother for, and she still considered Aveline her mother despite what she knew now. But Jess wouldn't hold the things Pawpaw did over Aveline's head. Not when she as much a victim as Lottie was, as Celia and Jess were. Not when she had killed the man to protect her children from him.

"That bastard left her rotting under the house all this time," Aveline spat. "She at least deserved to be buried properly. A grave where we could mourn, not trapped under a decaying house."

Jess' teeth dug into her bottom lip. There had been more than one reason as to why she decided to visit Aveline today rather than just say a quick hello during one of her shifts.

"Keith and Sam tore up the floor." Jess kept her voice low even though they were the only two on the porch. "They...they found her."

And Jess had received the phone call days ago, the tremble in Sam's voice telling her all she needed to know before she heard Keith's muted bawling in the background. Jess had waited until she ended the call before she curled up on the floor and sobbed for the thin woman chained under the house like a misbehaving dog by a cruel men that Jess tried so hard not to think about even though she still bore the marks—skeletal red fingerprints around her ankle—from where he had tried so desperately to drown her in the lake with him.

"Oh. Oh, Lottie..." her frail shoulders curled inward, and she held the bundle of yarn to her face to muffle the sobs.

Jess stood and carefully embraced Aveline, resting her cheek on Aveline's shoulder. "Let it out, Momma." Jess rubbed her back, blinking her own tears away. "Let it all out."

Jess cradled the cordless between her ear and her shoulder as she unpacked a box labeled KITCHEN in black marker in search of her coffee cups. The line trilled in her ear, and she waited for Celia to answer, finding several plates and a bowl, but not her cups. She was tired of drinking coffee out of plastic cups or a soup bowl—they had run out of plastic cups the night before—because she kept putting off packing. Part of her knew it was because she still couldn't get used to the fact that this place was hers.

A townhouse at the end of a row, an elderly couple on the other side and a sidewalk on the other. A few blocks one way and she would find a playground and a community pool. A few blocks the opposite way and there was a row of shops and a bar. If she walked out of her double doors to her modest, gated patio, she'd see the lake and the trails that wound around the glittering water. She had a perfect sized kitchen with a dining area, a living room that fit a sectional, a half bath tucked under the stairs with a full upstairs, and two bedrooms. Better yet, she fell asleep in Sam's arms every night and woke up to her in the morning.

Jess expected to wake up from her dream at any moment.

"Hello," Celia said.

"Finally," Jess huffed. "I thought you'd never pick up."

Celia sighed. "It only rang like five times, Jess. I was in the middle of cooking dinner."

"What are you making?"

"Spaghetti." There was a pause and a plastic scratching sound as Celia switched her phone from one ear to another. "Did you call to ask me what I'm making for dinner?"

Jess snorted. "No, I called to tell you I visited Momma today—"

"You work there."

"Not today, I didn't." She sighed in annoyance. "Can I finish my sentence?"

"Sorry, Jess."

"Anyway, I visited Ma today and apparently she's decided to crochet a blanket between today and Saturday."

Celia laughed "Well, it's Tuesday. She might have a chance of finishing it before the party. Are you sure we can stay in the guest room? I don't want to impose on you and Sam."

"It'll be fine. Sam got a blow-up mattress and some sleeping bags since we don't have a bed in there yet and it's just for the night." Jess finally found a coffee cup wrapped tight in newspaper. "If it's nice I thought the kids might like to hang around the pool for a bit or play on the playground. We even have a little charcoal grill outside that Sam's excited to use for the first time."

"A-are..." Celia trailed off and cleared her throat. "Are you settling in okay after...after everything?"

They hadn't really spoken about what happened. Jess had apologized when Sam told her about drugging Celia, but Celia seemed perfectly content to act as if nothing terrible had happened that night. As if her own sister hadn't tried to drug and potentially kill her. As if the ghost of their Pawpaw hadn't tried to drown Jess in the pond. Jess had yet to tell her about finding Lottie's remains under the house. Frankly, she wasn't sure Celia wanted to know.

"I'm fine." Jess winced at her knee-jerk response. "I'm doing good most of the time, at least. Therapy helps. Staying busy helps. Sam helps."

Celia sighed in relief. "Good. I'm glad, Jess, I really am."

Jess leaned against the counter. "Look, Celia, about what happened—"

"It's fine, Jess," Celia said, voice growing tight. "We don't...*I'd* prefer to leave things where they are on that. I've," —she drew in a shuddering breath— "I've put away a lot of things. Locked them away and buried them in the back of my head. Remembering and working through it seems to help you and I'm happy that you've found a way to deal with this, but I just prefer to forget. Is that okay?"

Jess nodded until she remembered Celia couldn't see her. "That's okay, Cel. Thank you for checking on me anyway."

Young voices erupted in the background and Celia sighed. "The kids have smelled dinner. I better get them fed so they can unwind before bed. We'll be there Saturday and we can catch up more then, yeah?"

"Yeah."

"Love you, Jess."

"Love you too."

Jess placed the cordless onto the counter and ran her fingers through her hair. Part of her hoped Celia would want to deal with this with her, but Jess understood her need to shove things into the dark recesses of her mind rather than look them in the face. If Jess could still do that without those things manifesting in hurtful ways, she would be content to never look at what had happened ever again. When Sam had first coaxed her to a therapy appointment, Jess thought she'd remain locked up tight, carrying the secrets she had learned to the grave. She had been terrified that honesty would land her right back in the hospital taking pills that didn't help her. But when Misty had asked Jess, "what would you like to accomplish in these sessions?" Jess had burst into tears, shocked that anyone but Sam would care about what she wanted.

With a sigh, she leaned her head back against the cabinet. The microwave blinked the time in neon green. Sam would be home any minute now covered in her usual machine oil and grease-stained coveralls and clunky work boots that she would kick off on the tile foyer so they wouldn't ruin their beige carpet they planned to keep clean for as long as possible. Keith had been sad to see his daughter leave his shop but thrilled that she had finally decided to get the hell out of that backwards town, and that she had chosen a city only a few hours away. Juniper and Keith helped them find the place and move in, promising to visit as often as possible since Jess wasn't sure how long it would take before she could set foot back in Marisville. The months she had spent in Sam's trailer, barely leaving except to go to Sam's parents, hadn't been terrible but she didn't want to repeat them.

Jess' eyes fluttered closed, as she waited for the telltale scratch of Sam's key in the lock and the slight catch as the door opened.

Drip, drip, drip.

Her eyes flew open. Fear gripped her quivering heart in its icy fingers and squeezed. Jess' breath rattled in her lungs. No. This couldn't be happening. Not again. She wouldn't let him take her. Shaky legs carried her out of the kitchen and into the living room. Shadows loomed thick in heavy in the corners of the room. When had it gotten so dark? She peered into the darkness, expecting the rotting shadow with its fat wriggling worms to glide across her carpet and attempt to take her over again. Perhaps it would make her walk the trail around the lake before coaxing her underneath its cold waters.

"Leave me alone," she demanded, her voice wobbling. "I won't go with you! I won't—"

The metallic scraping of a key entering a lock. Rubber catching slightly as a door opened. The light clicked on above the foyer.

"Baby why are you standing in the dark?" Sam asked, closing the door behind her and tossing her keys onto a small table.

Jess' eyes darted around the room, searching for the shadows that had dispelled as soon as the light clicked on. "I...I thought I..." she bit back a small sob. "I heard dripping and—"

The acrid stench of machine oil assaulted her nose, but she couldn't care less as she sank into Sam's embrace, letting her lover hold her tightly. Enough to know that this was real. She wasn't dreaming or hallucinating. She was real and she was still her.

"I'll check the faucets okay. Something may need tightening, that's all," Sam murmured in Jess' ear, fingers digging into Jess' back. "You're safe. You're here with me."

Jess nodded, pressing her face into the crook of Sam's neck. Her eyes flitted to the small, ornate, gold-framed mirror they had found at a flea market because Jess thought it was perfect for the foyer.

Lottie stared back.

About the author

Luna Fiore is a genderfluid speculative fiction author from Eastern North Carolina with a MFA in Creative Writing from SNHU. WHERE WILLOWS WEEP is his debut horror, but he is also the author of dark fantasy series, The Underhill Saga. She's dreamed of other worlds since she was a child making potions out of mud, sticks, and roly-polys. When he isn't writing he is playing in video game worlds and corralling her small zoo of three cats and two St. Bernards.

Also by Luna Fiore